I0682371

Speak to Me

Mute, witty and dangerous

N. I. Smith

First published in the UK in 2013 by Newnat Books

13 digit ISBN 978 0992 654610

A CIP catalogue record for this title is available from the British Library.

N.I. Smith

To Maresa

Chapter 1

Mum opens the van doors and guides my chair into the back of the van. I'm fourteen. This is my first day of mainstream school. Mum's nervous, it's just as well I'm strapped in! We go racing down the hill and stop opposite the university. This is where I want to be. I want to study English but I don't know what school's going to be like.

A green bus comes alongside. I can see the boys in blazers like mine.

'Hey boys,' I think, 'I'm coming to your school.'

Spit runs down my chin. Then my stomach does a flip and I start to panic. They're all staring at me with their mouths open.

I'm not stupid. We pass the sign for the school, a girl holding her brother's hand. How long will it be before I get to hold a boy's hand?

The van bounces over the speed bumps. It makes me call out. Mum reverses into the disabled bay. Everyone's staring at me as Mum opens the back doors.

Speak to me.

A cool breeze blew across my face as Mum wheeled me out.

"Oh."

Two boys were walking up the drive towards me. The taller one flicked his fringe out of his eyes. He caught my eye and I wondered why he was moving his hands about so fast. His friend, with fair hair and glasses, listened patiently.

Mum activated the tail lift and I floated downwards. The metal plates clanked on the tarmac.

"Look out, the daleks are coming," said the boy with the fringe.

Wanker. You can leave out the sarky comments. But there was something in his voice, like the first taste of watermelon in summer. Speak to me.

Leaves whirled around me. Mum locked up the van and drove my chair up the ramp. Warm air greeted me as we went through the automatic doors and Mum reversed the chair against the wall opposite reception. She took my woollen beret off and spoke to the receptionist.

The doors opened to let more people in and several car horns tooted angrily. Mum patted my shoulder.

"I'll just move the van, someone's going to stay with you."

She went outside.

The entrance hall reminded me of all the schools I'd been in before: the noise, the hats being snatched and thrown about, the threats:

"You tramp, I'll get you for that," bums and crotches of so many different races.

I noticed everyone's hands and lower halves as they squeezed past the bottleneck created by my wheelchair. Would any of these boys actually speak to me?

I had daydreamed about a boy who was bright and not bookish, sporty and not competitive and playful, very playful. The boy's face morphed between black, white, mixed race and Asian. He might be one of the thirty odd people in my new class for all I knew. His voice would be deep and he'd laugh at my jokes; I wouldn't have to explain myself or apologise.

"Hello, I'm Jennifer," a girl my age had steered across the stream of people coming in through the entrance and crouched down in front of me. "I'm the volunteer on reception today."

Jennifer, can you see me smiling at you, with your freckles and your thick ginger hair? A sea of trousers washed past us.

"What's your name?"

My elbows rose and my head swung from side to side. A frown appeared over Jennifer's hazel eyes. She pouted. An ear-shattering bell rang and my legs tensed up.

"Ow," said Jennifer. She looked at the clock. "Is someone coming?"

Where are you, Mum? I don't want to be late on my first day and where's Becky?

"You look hot," Jennifer stroked the hair out of my eyes, took off my mittens and unwound my scarf. "You've got lovely hair," she said.

She leaned over and put the mittens and scarf in my backpack at the back of the chair. Boobs: I bet the boys like you, Jennifer. Becky rushed in through the doors.

"Hi Lauren, sorry I'm late. The bus was blocking the way. I saw your mum."

Jennifer stood up and pointed to her name badge. "Hi, I'm helping on reception. Do you know where Lauren's meant to be this morning?"

"Ten D with Mr Preston."

Jennifer turned and looked down at me. "You're in my class."

I felt warm inside; Jennifer had smiled when she spoke to me. Becky signed in and got out a red clipboard from the shoulder bag on the right of my chair. It had a laminated 'Qwerty' keyboard printed on it. She held my hand over the board. I was too tense at first. I thought about the cherry tree in our garden which flowers in spring. My hand relaxed and my finger made tiny movements that Becky was able to exaggerate so that I could tap out a series of letters on the board.

T-h-a-n-k y-o-u f-o-r

"Thank you for – " said Becky. The swirling mass of young people began to drain away down the corridors.

s-t-a-y-i-n-g w-i-t-h m-e J-e-n-n-i-f-e-r.

- staying with me, Jennifer.

"Wow, that's cool," said Jennifer.

My finger tapped some more.

I'm glad you're in my class.

"So am I," said Jennifer.

You made me feel very welcome. Thank you.

"Aww," Jennifer's cheeks coloured.

Mum came back in, her frizzy hair sticking out more than usual. "Sorry, that took ages," she said. "Right, Lauren, are you all set for your first day?" She looked at me and squeezed my hand then she leaned over and kissed me on the cheek.

Stop it, Mum, I'm not a baby.

Mum hugged Becky. "I hope it all goes well. I'll see you at twelve thirty. Bye."

Enjoy it, Mum, I'm off your hands for three hours. Jennifer led the way down the empty corridor. Becky switched on my chair and we began to roll. My heart jumped into the back of my throat. I watched Jennifer's hair billowing out behind her. We turned right and then left down a series of dark corridors lined with lockers and passed lots of doors until we came to the moment of truth.

Jennifer stopped at the door with a white plastic sign: '10D'.

Becky got the comb out, ran it through my hair and whispered in my ear:

"This is it, Lauren, the start of Year Ten."

Jennifer opened the classroom door and a wall of sound reached my ears: thirty odd boys and girls shouting and arguing. The noise level rose as Jennifer went in and died away as soon as Becky followed me in.

The wheels of my chair squeaked on the lino floor as Becky manoeuvred towards a table nearest the teacher's chair which was empty.

I could feel everyone's eyes on me while they held their breath.

Becky broke the silence.

"Can I move this table forward a bit?"

A girl with long brown hair and thick glasses shrugged her shoulders. Becky lifted and scraped the table, which grated on my ears. She pushed a chair out of the way and fitted me in with difficulty in the narrow space.

I picked up a few comments as people started talking again.

"Oh no, this is going to slow us all down."

"Good, I might get some homework done in school time."

The sound level began to rise. I happened to turn my head and caught sight of the boy who made the dalek comment.

"Oi've gort lurrning needs," he grunted.

Bang, the sound of a chair being kicked.

"Shut up. She's probably brighter than you are," that was Jennifer.

I wanted to thank her and I wanted her to be my friend forever. In came a man with thinning blond hair carrying a heavy case.

"Good morning, I'm Mr Preston, your form teacher for this year. I think I've met most of you before." He gave a long meaningful stare towards the boys at the back. I distantly remembered meeting him on my first visit to the school. "We have a new student in class today and she's here with her learning support assistant."

Becky stood up and twizzled my chair round to face the class. Blank, bored and frankly hostile faces stared at me or pointedly looked out of the window so they didn't have to notice me.

"Thank you, Mr Preston, I'm Becky, Lauren's LSA. Lauren wants to say hello and how much she's looking forward to meeting you all."

Bollocks. I hated everyone except Jennifer. I wanted to be somewhere else.

"She's had a home tutor until now."

I often feel patronised by my carers. My adrenaline levels peaked. Mr Preston spoke up:

"I know you'll all look after Lauren and make her feel welcome."

About as welcome as a fish being introduced to the crocodiles.

"We've got five minutes for you to ask her any questions and you'll see how she communicates."

I scanned the twenty seven faces of different races all staring at me. Jennifer smiled but I couldn't help noticing the troubled, disgusted and angry looks on everyone else's faces. Would I be able to do FC at all?

My hair swung about as my head wobbled from side to side. I drooled down my chin. Becky held up the clipboard.

"This way of speaking is called Facilitated Communication, or 'FC'."

"Any questions?" said Mr Preston.

There was a chorus of 'Sir, sir.'

Mr Preston pointed to a boy near the back.

"Yes, Dan."

Dan tilted his head and smirked.

"How old is she?"

"You need to ask Lauren," said Becky.

"How old are you?"

Becky brought a chair over and sat down.

There were a few giggles and whispered remarks that I didn't catch while I was tapping on the board.

"I'm fifteen in January," said Becky.

Dan raised his eyebrows and looked away.

"Sir, sir."

"Anthony," said Mr Preston.

So it was Anthony who had the fringe and who'd made the comment about daleks.

"How do you manage without words, Lauren?"

I can't remember a time before words.

He leaned over and sniggered something to the boy next to him. What's your problem, Anthony? Then it was his friend's turn.

"Yes Matt, go ahead."

"Do loud noises affect you?"

Good question.

Yes. My ears are very sensitive. Loud noises make my muscles go tight.

Matt narrowed his eyes thoughtfully.

The girl sitting on my table was called Emily

"Where do you live?" she asked.

Landsley Park.

That raised a few eyebrows. We have a big detached house on a private road.

CRASH!

An ear-shattering bomb blast filled the room and echoed around the walls.

I screamed. My fists went rose to shoulder level and both my legs kicked out. It was excruciating in front of the whole class.

"Sorry, sir," said Anthony, "it was an accident."

Bastard. Anthony picked up a book from the floor that had somehow slid off his table. Why had I ever thought I wanted to speak to you?

"Okay, settle down now," said Mr Preston. "Every Friday we'll have a tutorial and all of you will have a chance to help Lauren communicate."

Becky turned my chair round and tried to fit my feet back under the table; they wouldn't go. She parked my chair at the side of the room.

"Right, later on this term, we're going to be studying a character in a horror story. I want you to start by thinking about your favourite characters: it may be from a film, a computer game or a book. Who's your favourite character and why?"

"Yes, Anthony?"

"CP30," he continued in a robot voice "'we seem to be made to suffer, it's our lot in life'."

The boys laughed. It was a clever imitation; he sounded like Stephen Hawking.

"Oh."

I wanted to speak. Mr Preston must have heard me but he paid no attention. Lots of people got chosen before me. So this is how it's going to be, is it? I carried on calling out.

"Lara Croft from Tomb Raider," said Jennifer.

"Yes," said several voices.

Mr Preston picked out Dan and Emily and finally turned to Becky.

"Yes, Lauren?"

Lyra in Northern Lights, because she's brave.

"Yes I like her too," said Emily.

That morning I had the same agonising introductions in maths and history.

The teachers looked non-plussed and the boys and girls in my classes looked bored and unfriendly. Once I understood what I needed to do, the work wasn't that difficult. The bell rang at the end of the morning and Becky collected my books and pens together.

"How did I do?" she said.

Fine.

Becky knew how crap I felt but I wasn't going to say that. Becky was a good friend and much too well-meaning to have to cope with all the shit I'd had.

I liked her. I couldn't work with anyone I didn't like. She'd taken notes, opened the books at the right pages and kept an eye out for me when I wanted to speak or ask a question but she didn't get everything right.

I could murder someone out of frustration when people like Anthony were mean to me. I had to get through those awful first few days in the hope that things would settle down and I'd cope with the comments and prehistoric attitudes.

Mum visited at lunch time and spooned a beef stew into my mouth. I was hungry and there was still the afternoon to come.

Julian took over from Becky.

"Hi Lauren," he said when he met me in the corridor, "how is Princess Leia on her first day?"

Sick of Star Wars.

"Nah."

Julian wasn't listening. Anthony stopped by my chair. His Adam's apple stood out because of his long neck. He was wriggly and random.

"Afraid I was going to leave without a goodbye kiss?" he said.

Some kind of quote from the film.

"That's right," said Julian, "no one hates Star Wars, it's not possible."

It is. Julian looked up and down the corridor which made his ponytail swing from side to side.

"Which way is the science lab?"

"This way," said Anthony, "that's where I'm going."

We followed Anthony.

Alll along the way I could pick up the smell of his aftershave. It was like a fox hunt. We entered the science lab which was fitted out with Bunsen burners, goggles and white coats. A list of instructions was projected onto the whiteboard, including:

'Form a group of three to plot a cooling curve. Each person to take one role:
a: keep time
b: take readings of temperature every 60 seconds
c: draw up a graph and enter the readings.'

Julian joined Anthony and Matt at the back.
"Hi guys, can we join you?"
"If you like," said Anthony. He creased up his nose like a girl. There were a few freckles on either side of his nose. "She can't do much, can she?"
"You'd be surprised," said Julian and turning to me, "she notices things all the time, don't you, Lauren?"
I kept noticing Anthony. Why do I keep bumping into you?
You don't like me; you've made that clear enough.
"It's okay," said Matt, "I'll do the timing as well as the recording."
Julian fetched a thermometer and Matt filled a metal cylinder full of boiling water and brought it over to the bench beside the sink.
"This is like the Government telling us all what to think," said Julian.
He got chatting with Matt in the intervals between taking readings. Anthony was drawing with a biro on a spare piece of graph paper.

"Arthur C Clarke," said Julian, "he was the greatest scientist. He recognised how much trouble computers would bring."

"Are you talking about science fiction?" said Matt, "Kraken by China Melville is the best."

I'd read lots of science fiction and I raised my arm so Julian would see I wanted to speak. He paid no attention so I concentrated on listening. I was going to learn different things in the afternoon when Julian was around.

"Matt and I went on a bird race to campaign against the ring road," said Anthony.

"I didn't know about that," said Julian, "did you win?"

"No, a bunch of Bill Oddie lookalikes from Derby won it. They got fifty six species."

The timer rang so Matt leaned over the apparatus.

"Sixty five point three degrees Celsius," he said.

"It doesn't have to be that accurate," said Anthony as he filled a box in the table and marked a point on the graph.

"But we saw forty one species," said Matt.

"That's good," said Julian, "in twenty four hours?"

"Just twelve," said Anthony, "someone saw a shore lark by the sandstone quarry."

Julian turned to me and noticed my raised arm. He picked up the board and held my hand over the letters. Anthony put down his biro and stared at my fingers while I did the FC.

He probably thought it was a big beach.

Anthony smiled broadly, "Yeah," he said. "Did Lauren just say that?"

"That's right," said Julian.

"That's amazing."

Don't laugh. Just because I can't speak doesn't mean I'm stupid. I decided to be polite.

Can I see your drawing, Anthony?

Anthony's jaw dropped.

He looked genuinely gobsmacked that I could spell out his name. He picked up the paper he'd been drawing on and held it up right in front of my face. I recognised the figure immediately.

It's Mr Preston. That's brilliant.

It wasn't perfect but he'd captured the tired smile that our English teacher had at the end of the lesson.

"Thanks," he said, peering deep into my eyes while his eyes were smiling.

I felt confused that the boy who seemed to hate me should look at me like that. He was probably studying me so he could copy my movements and imitate me. But his next question surprised me.

"Can you see okay, Lauren?" he said.

"Anthony," said the teacher, "why is it always you talking when people are trying to concentrate?"

Dan turned round from the bench in front of us.

"Yeah, shut up, Ant," he said, loud enough for Anthony to hear but not the teacher. Dan's friends sniggered and one of them gave Anthony the finger.

Anthony turned his drawing over and stared down at the blank graph paper. I felt sorry for him and upset because we were just starting to have a conversation. Julian might be okay. He didn't make many notes and I couldn't read his scrawly writing but he might be more help in making friends with the boys.

Mum collected me at the end of the day. She operated the tail lift and I rose vertically up in the air.

My first day had been uninterrupted stress apart from those few moments with Jennifer when I arrived and when Anthony showed me his drawing.

Silly questions circled in my head like buzzards: why did Anthony take such a lot of notice of Dan? Why had he asked about my eyes?

I got no further in answering them. I needed peace. Unfamiliar boys' voices and laughter rang in my ears. I was never going to fit in. I was never going to make any friends. My big hope was the tutorial that Mr Preston had set up.

Crowded, noisy schooldays alternated with quiet evenings at home. Becky came to my house every evening to do an hour's homework. The pattern of my week became clear: Mondays, Thursdays and Fridays were full days and I finished at lunch time on Tuesday and Wednesday.

Friday first lesson was set aside for a tutorial with me.

"Where do you want to go, Lauren?" said Mr Preston.

That simple question was so important.

By the window.

I needed the natural light.

Becky and the classroom assistant arranged two tables by the radiator which looked out onto the football pitch and a row of houses. I liked the thought that blackbirds would be collecting worms outside while I was getting to know the boys and girls in my class.

Mr Preston chose ten people to join me to watch FC in action.

I hadn't realised how nervous I'd be. It took ages to get everyone settled at the tables, there was less and less time left. Becky showed how I could play noughts and crosses by pointing to where I wanted my 'x' to go. Dan tried to guide my hand but with all the excitement and everyone watching it was impossible for me to relax. My hand wouldn't move until Dan wrestled it across the board.

"Gently," said Becky, "wait for Lauren to help."

Dan tried again for half a minute.

"It's no good," he said, "it won't go."

I'm not a machine. You need to tune in to my wavelength.

The rest of the class was supposed to be setting targets for the coming year but they were all watching Dan instead. Mr Preston came over and spoke quietly to Becky. She came and sat beside me and Mr Preston returned with pencils and a stack of paper.

"Now let's try something different. Take one sheet of paper each and draw a picture of something you'll be using at the weekend."

Dan gave Jake a dig in the ribs and smirked. Everyone scribbled away on the paper.

"Has everyone done that?"

There were nods of agreement.

"Now, starting with you, Dan, show the picture to Lauren and see if she can tell what it is."

Dan showed me his picture. It was a strange oval shape with a cross in the middle and circles either side.

Console.

"Not just any console," he said, "it's a Nintendo DS."

Mr Preston turned his attention to the rest of the class.

"Who else has a drawing?" said Becky.

Emily did a drawing of the cage she kept her mouse in. Matt showed me a picture of his ice hockey boots. Anthony held up his drawing but I couldn't work out what it was. It looked like a candle or Blackpool tower. He wouldn't say what it was.

"That's crap," said Dan and everyone laughed.

Anthony blushed and went silent. At the end of the lesson Becky and Mr Preston congratulated each other on having devised a game on the spur of the moment.

"Perfect," said Mr Preston. I wasn't sure. I didn't like the way the boys talked to each other.

I fell asleep in the lounge that evening. Mum had tipped the chair back to make it more comfortable. The light from the TV flickered on the ceiling. It was a cooking competition. I called out and Mum came across.

"Are you alright, Lauren?" she said, yawning. She put the light on and picked up my hand.

I'm in pain.

Mum leaned me forwards and adjusted the cushions.

"You've been sweating. You must be worn out."

Mum adjusted my chair, switched off the TV and went out to get me a drink. My first week in school felt like an unmitigated disaster. I had no idea how I was doing. I tried to think of the good things: Jennifer had been kind on my first day but she'd kept away from me since then. Emily who sat next to me smiled once but ignored me apart from that. The only other person who paid me the slightest attention was Anthony and I didn't trust him. And yet in that moment in science it seemed as if he was about to come out of his shell. Why did I feel upset about the way Dan made fun of him? It's just how boys are.

Chapter 2

"Anthony, would you read for us?"

The school day was nearly over when Anthony got called forward in English. His was the last voice I'd wanted to hear. He'd shown an active dislike of me from the moment when I first arrived at school.

He stood and stretched and the bones in his spine cracked. I hated those sounds. He hunched his shoulders and walked past me like a prisoner who'd been forced to volunteer.

"Frankenstein, chapter five," said Mr Preston. Anthony sat on a chair at the front facing us all. "Page fifty six. Here's where the real story begins."

Anthony took a deep breath and looked at me.

"'It was on a dreary night in November, that I beheld the accomplishment of my toils…'"

Anthony's voice was on the point of breaking so the pitch alternated between high notes and breathier low notes. Maybe that's why he was so self conscious. I thought: 'you're the most prejudiced person in my class.'

He took in a sentence and looked up as he read about Victor's horror at the wretch he'd made. Anthony began to concentrate more and more on me. I felt his anger as he spat out the insulting references to the hideous countenance of the cripple.

I tried to return his gaze but my head kept swinging towards the window. Anthony made no secret of it; he was reading the stream of archaic expressions of disgust and anxiety directly at me.

Mr Preston had talked about identifying with the characters.

I'd become the ugly and disturbing creature, the accident of nature. I was part of Anthony's captive audience and he was attacking my right to be in the classroom.

As he read on, the tone of his voice changed. He stirred something inside me and the rhythm of his reading lulled me into a kind of trance. He paused and turned to Mr Preston who made a circle with his finger, meaning: 'Carry on.' A stillness fell over the class while Anthony read honestly from the heart. Every trace of pain and pretence vanished. His voice was quite distinct from the sarcastic copycat voice he normally put on. A gentle drizzle tapped on the windows and erased the trees beyond the playground and a dusky light crept into the room.

He read about the frightful fiend that 'doth close behind him tread'. Victor dreaded to return home in case the dreadful monster was lingering in his bedroom. Some time later, Anthony reached the end of the chapter and turned to Mr Preston. No one moved except me; I gave an involuntary shiver. I wanted to hear more. Minutes passed before Mr Preston spoke.

"Excellent," that was all he said.

Anthony walked back between the tables. My elbow lifted up on its own and poked him in the ribs as he passed by.

"Ow."

"Don't worry," said Becky, "it wasn't deliberate."

It was. What do you really think about me? I want to know.

Mr Preston switched on the light and spoke about Mary Shelley and Science. Then the bell rang. Everyone stood up and started putting their books away.

"Read the next three chapters for next week," said Mr Preston.

Call Anthony over.

Becky shouted: "Anthony,"

But he paid no attention; Jennifer was already talking to him.

Let's barge in.

Becky guided my chair around the tables and parked between Anthony and Jennifer. Mr Preston waved as he went by.

"Well done, Anthony," he said, "you seem to have made a new friend."

Anthony frowned. Becky caught hold of my hand so I could speak. My finger spelt out a string of expletives. I'd got overexcited; I couldn't clear my head. I didn't know what was happening

"What's that, Lauren?" said Anthony.

Becky refused to read out my words. I was sure Anthony must have read them anyway.

You were Victor.

"You noticed." He beamed at me and it was the most disarming and wholehearted smile I'd seen. He knew what I meant. He turned away and walked out of the room with Matt.

As he went through the doorway he parroted Mr Preston's words: "Three chapters for next week."

Why did you have to put on voices all the time?

Mr Preston gave me and Becky the freedom to use the twenty minute Friday sessions for whatever we chose. We played guessing games but we had to do everything quietly because everyone else was trying to study. I missed hearing people's voices. I didn't learn much about the boys in my class.

I used up a lot of nervous anxiety trying to do FC which left me tired for the rest of the day. I wanted people to come up to me and just chat but that wasn't happening.

No one speaks to me.

"I know," said Becky after lunch one day, "give it time. I'm sure they will."

Everything went on around me in the school corridors which were like underground tunnels, poorly lit and diverting this way and that.

I couldn't join in because everyone was standing while I was sitting and things happened too quickly. Teachers patrolled constantly:

"Where's your tie, Robert? Tuck your shirt in, Joseph."

The boys behaved like chimpanzees. Dan and his friends ran about, pushing each other and hiding stuff, all the while eating and swearing and insulting the girls. The girls hung out with their friends and picked on people who didn't fit in. Someone took Emily's glasses but Jennifer got them back. No one picked on me but I watched school life in the corridors with growing horror. I was on the outside.

Weeks passed and I began to despair of any of my schoolmates tuning into my wavelength and learning FC.

I'd become accepted but only as an obstacle in the middle of the corridor. People didn't stare as much; they stepped around my chair as if I was a phantom. It was beginning to get to me.

Three weeks in and things weren't so bad. Becky brought me inside to finish my maths homework.

"Why equals two ex plus three," said Becky.

We'd tried sitting outside under the pergola among the vines and honeysuckle but the breeze made it impossible to enjoy the evening sun. Becky parked my chair at the dining table facing the garden. She read out the questions from the worksheet that Mr Todd had set that day.

"Ex equals why over two minus one."

It was a new language. I concentrated hard to hold these strange terms in my head.

Becky's voice made some of the strings of Mum's piano resonate.

"Where do they intersect? Okay, starting with the first one. Where does it hit the why axis?"

I pointed to the number 3.

"No, Lauren," said Becky, "you need to spell out the number. Then I can be sure that you've worked it out for yourself."

Three.

Becky wrote up the answers in my exercise book. I watched the evening primrose plants swaying in the wind and saw myself reflected in the mirror above the mantelpiece.

I liked maths; it was pointless but satisfying, a bit like juggling. As long as I kept the figures in my head it was easy.

I started thinking about what a bird race was and my answers came out all wrong.

"We'll do some more later," said Becky.

Thank goodness for that. I drank a blackcurrant milk shake through a straw. Becky read out a piece about the First World War and then asked a series of questions. I enjoyed listening carefully and finding the right answer. It wasn't hard. I was getting 'A's in English, history and maths.

Doors were opening. School was delivering on the academic side, showing me that I was doing as well as everyone else in the subjects I cared about.

I didn't do so well in science and French. Darkness fell outside, smells drifted through from the kitchen where Mum was baking a pie.

The windows of the Maths classroom looked out onto a neglected courtyard and a brick wall. Mr Todd's style was to bury his black framed glasses in the maths book, run his hand through his almost white blond hair and read out passages in a transatlantic accent. We were supposed to fill in the gaps:

"Where's Jake – playing hookey again?"

"It's a dental appointment," said Liz.

"Okay. Simultaneous equations: 'The method used to solve simultaneous equations is – ', Lauren?"

I had no idea what he was talking about. He used a projector which had an irritating rattle that made my ear drums vibrate. It flickered a lot so I couldn't take in the text we were supposed to be using to answer the questions.

"Elimination, come on, get with the program. Two equations are simplified by, Daniel? "

"Err - subtraction?"

"That's right."

I found myself concentrating on the half erased words on the whiteboard. Later on, Mr Todd handed out our exercise books.

"Jennifer, sixty eight per cent, well done, show your working out, Jake, fifty two per cent, you missed out three questions, Emily, eighty eight percent, keep it up. Lauren - "

He paused as if it was a reality game show.

"One hundred percent."

I was pretty sure I'd done well but I was delighted to hear I'd got full marks. Emily got called a creep because she always put her work in on time. That's what people might have called me.

At the end of our science lesson, Anthony sat on a stool next to me. Julian stopped putting my things away and got the board out.

"What does your Dad do?"

He left us. I live with my Mum.

What a stupid question. He deserted Mum when I was born.

"Sorry," Anthony hunched up his shoulders.

Then I was left feeling upset.

What does your Dad do?

"He works in a lab at the University."

Julian suddenly came to life.

"What, in the animal labs on the top floor?"

"I'm not sure exactly."

Ask him.

I don't know why I said that. Maybe it was Julian who was champing at the bit to find out.

"Okay, I will," said Anthony.

Becky handed my maths homework in early. It was all about powers and square roots. What sort of special powers would I like? I wanted Anthony to hear me and understand. I wanted to feel equal with him, not special or different, just equal. I wanted us to laugh at each other's jokes; not asking much really.

Julian took me outside at the end of the day and we waited by the bike shed for Mum to come.

Late as usual. Anthony saw me and came over. He crouched down beside my chair.

"I asked Dad about his job," he said.

Julian butted in:

"Yeah, and?" He didn't get the board out.

"He's doing an insect project. Fruit flies," said Anthony, "about mating preferences."

"Sounds mad," said Julian.

"Maybe, this experiment was supposed to find out whether the male fruit flies prefer females who're good at flying."

"What, is he going for a 'useless science' award?"

"I don't know. Anyway the experiment didn't work."

"What do you mean?"

"The wingless females mate as often as the winged ones."

"I suppose they can't get away."

"No, there was no preference either way. The males didn't care whether the females could fly or not."

Quite right, I thought, they all need to have sex.

"Weird," said Julian, "does he visit the animal house?"

"I dunno, probably, why do you ask?"

"No reason," said Julian.

No reason at all. Julian was itching to know the security codes so he and his mates could break in and rescue the animals but Anthony couldn't see that.

Becky sneezed during Mr Todd's maths class the following week.

"Probably all the viruses flying round the school," she said.

She wasn't multi-tasking seamlessly like she normally did. Meanwhile I couldn't get my head round common denominators. Mr Todd was making allowances but he frowned at me.

"I don't understand how you do so well in homework when you haven't answered a single question correctly in class."

It took a moment for his words to sink in. What? Are you suggesting I cheat? I raised my arm to show Becky I wanted to speak. I wanted to scream but I held myself back.

"Becky, did you study maths at college?"

"No, I did Psychology at uni," said Becky, "we only did a little statistics."

"Oh, well," said Mr Todd, combing his hair with his right hand.

Becky put her pen down and stood up. The whole class woke up. Everyone turned to Becky who walked to the front and pointed her finger at Mr Todd.

"Excuse me," she said loudly, "are you suggesting that I've done the homework and not Lauren?"

Mr Todd's whole body jolted.

"Woah there, calm down,"

"I'm not a horse – "

"I was just – "

"Because if that's what you think – "

Becky was out of the door before Mr Todd had a chance to reply, leaving me completely on my own. When my helpers get upset I suffer more than they do. Becky was right but it was me who was being attacked. I was furious and I had no chance to speak.

Mr Todd called the classroom assistant over and left the room.

I was frantic, trying to make out the raised voices in the corridor over the exchange of comments in the classroom. Anthony and Dan thought it was a big laugh.

Everyone seemed to be enjoying this scene except me. I could hear Becky's high pitched tones but I couldn't tell what she was saying.

When she came back in she was drying her eyes with a tissue. Mr Todd followed soon after. I wished the lesson would finish.

"Quiet now," he said and picked up the last book. "Anthony," he looked up and searched for Anthony's face. "Fifty percent, barely adequate. If you need help, just ask."

Anthony came forward to pick up his exercise book but as he lifted it up it fell apart. On the inside cover was a drawing of a girl with her arms in the air.

I didn't get a close look but I recognised the black hair, the chair and the board; it was me. Anthony sheepishly fitted the pages together. He knew I'd seen it.

Let's go home.

"But we've got science next," said Becky.

Just call Mum.

Mum brought me home. I was too upset to do any physics. Mr Todd had climbed to the top of my hate list of teachers. He had no idea what he'd done.

I chose to sit upstairs in my study which was a mistake. Mum put a talking book on but I couldn't follow the story. I looked at the rows of books and DVD's, the computer and the communication devices.

None of it was any use when I felt hopeless. I dreaded losing my way in school. Why had everything turned out so bad when I'd put so much effort in?

There was a mug on the windowsill which I'd had made during an inclusion conference. 'Together we'll get there,' it said in pink letters. Fat chance.

I sat watching the lights come on over town feeling utterly alone and locked in; the nightmare of understanding everything that was going on around me but having no way to let people know.

I felt I was back to square one: complete isolation, being cut off from the lives of everyone else my age.

All the promises the school had made, all the allowances and the preparation had come to nothing at all. The talking book carried on playing long after I stopped listening.

Mum and Becky were having a furious row downstairs.

I only caught occasional phrases but what I could make out made my heart sink.

"Find someone else," Becky had said and: "I can't cope."

I screamed.

It was all I could do at moments like that. No one came for a while. I sat in my study mentally throwing darts at the trunk of the cherry tree outside. I felt all of Becky's justified anger and all of Mum's upset concentrating inside me. Eventually Mum came upstairs.

"Have you slid down the chair?" She sounded upset. She adjusted the angle of the back rest and checked the belt that held me in place.

Take me downstairs.

Mum made a face.

"I didn't want to involve you in all this," she said.

Don't be ridiculous. How can I not be involved?

I need to talk to Becky.

"I don't think it will make any difference, Lauren," said Mum.

For God's sake, she's threatening to leave me which will be like the end of school forever.

I've got something to say to her.

Mum huffed and then adjusted the armchair so it would fit inside the lift. The three of us sat in silence around the dining room table.

You want to leave, Becky?

"That's not what I said; I don't want to. I can't cope with teachers undermining my - "

She rested her elbows on the table and hid her face behind her hands. She can't cope with me, I thought.

"Don't be like that, Becky," said Mum, "we'll never find an LSA who's as good as you."

I'm driving Becky mad. She spoke through her fingers.

"He's accusing me of cheating."

It's me he's accusing. He's attacking my right to speak and my right to learn. I hated Mr Todd. He was wrecking my whole future. He was blocking the gateway between me and university.

"I'm not going in there ever again," said Becky.

It's Mr Todd's fault.

"Stupid man," said Mum. "It's not working. You're not happy, are you, Lauren?"

Ouch. No, I'm in despair about coping at school but I'm not giving up yet.

We need a meeting.

Becky looked up.

"What good would that do?"

It's only Mr Todd. Everyone else is OK.

Well, kind of.

Mr Preston tries to help but the tutorials aren't really working and the other teachers do what they can. Nobody does enough.

Phone the school.

"It's half past four. There won't be anyone there," said Mum

*Phone the ****ing school.*

"Now stop it, Lauren," said Mum. "That's not going to help. What do you think, Becky?"

"It won't make the slightest difference," she said, hiding her face again.

To Mum's great credit she called the school's number, put the phone on speaker and held my hand so I could do FC.

"Hello," it was Trish, the school secretary.

Hello, it's Lauren Stark.

"Hello Mrs Stark," said Trish, "how can I help?"

Listen to me, you idiot.

Can I speak to Mr Trimble please?

"He's busy at the moment, can I ask what it's about?"

That bastard, Mr Todd.

"It's about Lauren's maths teacher," said Mum.

"Mr Trimble can call you back, perhaps - tomorrow afternoon."

I need a meeting now.

"We'd like to meet as soon as possible please," said Mum.

"I'm sorry, Mrs Stark, he's busy all day tomorrow."

**** *off. I'm not coming in to school until it's sorted out.*

"It's serious. I'm afraid Lauren's going to be staying off school until we can have a meeting."

"Is she ill?"

"No, she's upset."

"What about Monday?"

"No chance," said Trish, "he's much too busy."

Mum put the phone down.

"See," said Becky.

Phone Mr Hope.

Mum kept at it. She got through to Mr Hope at five to five. He was, the 'Senco': the Special Educational Needs Coordinator at the Education Authority. He promised to get a meeting together as soon as possible.

Mum and Becky looked at each other.

"You don't let anyone stand in your way, do you, Lauren?" said Becky.

Becky gave me a long hug before she left.

"I'm sorry, Lauren," she said.

She banged the front door louder than usual.

I stayed home on Friday and Mr Hope called to say we'd be meeting at the school at eight thirty on Monday morning. I'd missed the Friday tutorial and I felt low all day.

No one talks to me.

"Julian said you spoke to some of the boys."

Weeks ago.

Yes, to Anthony who makes fun of people.

"What would you like for tea?" said Mum

I'm not hungry.

"Cheer up, Lauren, it's not the end of the world."

It was. I was staring at a lifetime of being unemployed in a wheelchair, a lifetime with nothing beyond being fed and washed and toileted like some domestic animal, all because I'd have no qualifications.

All the things I'd dreamed off: flying to Iceland, speaking to presidents, giving lectures at international conferences were crumbling into dust. I'd never have the chance to even try.

I'd spiralled down into the lonely place I knew from the past when I was powerless to speak. It was like being at the bottom of a well with just a tiny circle of light visible where I could make out scattered shapes. Years had gone by when I could read and spell long before anyone realised I could.

Anthony, Mr Todd, Trish hovered over me like spectres threatening to block any initiative I might have.

"No, stop," they shouted at me.

Chapter 3

We arrived at school on the following Monday at five past eight. A few people, mostly schoolgirls were waiting outside.

Mum rang the buzzer and blond-haired Trish came to the door and let us in. She was wearing a black and white mid-thigh dress as if she was attending a seventies disco. Her heels were so high she was practically on stilts.

"You can wait in the office if you like," she said.

"No, we'll wait for Becky here, thanks," said Mum.

We sat opposite reception, the same spot where I'd met Jennifer on my first day. I saw Anthony waiting with all the other people. Becky struggled through the crowd and buzzed the door and Trish let her in

"We're meeting through here," she said.

She hung up our coats and led us through the office to a room with a long table with six seats on either side: the Governors' Room. Mum moved the seats around so that my chair was in the middle and she and Becky sat on either side.

"Mr Hope says he's on his way," said Trish.

I was wearing my lime green polo neck, green cardigan and dark green trousers. It was good to be out of uniform; I felt less like a convict and more like myself. Mum wore a blue dress in place of her usual jersey and slacks, Becky wore a jumper and her smart jeans. There was a black and white photo of a past headmaster on the wall, looking grim.

Mr Hope came in, he was about seven feet tall.

Good, I thought, he'll be able to kick Mr Todd under the table if he doesn't come up with a sensible plan.

In came the opposing team: Mr Todd, Mr Preston, Trish and Mr Azim, art teacher who was head of year. I'd only seen him once before.

"Hello, Lauren," said Mr Hope. He went round the room introducing everyone for Mum's benefit. Julian came in late in shabby jeans and an 'Occupy' T shirt. Everyone else was kitted out in suits, except for Mr Azim who wore a bright orange sports jacket and a cravat.

Trish started taking notes straight away. The bare room and the table made me think of talks at the United Nations about Palestine where discussions went on and on and got nowhere.

"If you'd like to begin, Mrs Stark," said Mr Hope.

"I'll read out Lauren's statement," said Mum.

It was great watching Mum when she was in this mood.

"'There's a lot that's going right at school. I'm doing well in maths, history and English. Access to all the rooms is fine. I really appreciate the time Mr Preston has set aside for me to get to know my classmates. There is just one problem. Mr Todd doesn't believe that I've done my maths homework.'"

Mr Todd leaned forward and adjusted his glasses.

"That's not quite true," he said, "I simply meant that I wanted to be certain that it was all your own work. I apologise if I gave the impression that I was accusing your LSA of cheating."

Becky nodded.

"We often need to rule out plagiarism in coursework," said Mr Hope. "You wouldn't believe the number of parents who present their work in place of their children's."

"That's got nothing to do with this," said Mum. "Becky was insulted by Mr Todd's whole approach."

"Lauren," said Mr Hope, "what do you make of all this?"

Apologies are no ****ing use.

Mum wouldn't say the swearword so I tapped it out again.

"That's true," said Mr Hope, "Mr Todd?"

"Since my disagreement with Becky, I've spoken to Mr Preston, and he's given me some advice."

"Yes, Lauren," said Mr Preston, "I appreciate those comments. I admit I had my doubts about FC at first but I've watched you closely. I can see a difference when you're following what's being said."

I couldn't help smiling. I'd been worrying that everyone thought FC was fake and to hear my form teacher say those things meant a lot.

"There's a light in your eyes and you sit up straighter when you understand something. You have a troubled look that crosses your face for an instant when you don't. I see the effort that you put into concentrating and your personality comes across in your language."

It was obvious really but lots of people get put off by all my extra movements and don't notice these things. Whether Mr Todd really would pick them up was another matter. There was a pause. A bell rang and hundreds of trampling feet could be heard in the corridor.

Mr Preston spoke first: "Would it help if I extended the time you have to share with the other students in tutorials?"

Yes.

"Let's go round the table and see what comments people have," said Mr Hope, "starting with you, Lauren."

I've said all I want to say.

Mum went on about delivery vans parking outside the school entrance. Becky said she needed a break during the lunch hour. Julian suggested exchange visits to a special school. Mr Todd talked about varying his teaching methods. I watched the discussion sink into a murky swamp.

Everyone turned to Mr Azim; he'd been silent up to that point.

"I'd like to organise a group of people to meet and talk to you, Lauren, if you think that would help."

Mr Preston leaned back in his chair and shook his head.

"That's pretty much what we're already," he said.

"Okay, to summarise," said Mr Hope, "one: the school apologises for the upset to your LSA and to Lauren through the misunderstanding over Mr Todd's comments."

"Two: Mr Todd will closely monitor your learning in class and adjust his teaching accordingly and three: Mr Preston will extend Lauren's time with other students in weekly tutorials Mr Azim?"

"I shall organise a weekly get-together – "

"Weekly?" said Mr Preston, "are you sure?"

"Yes, starting after half term, if you'd like that, Lauren."

Yes I would.

"I can announce it in Assembly tomorrow so people can sign up straight away," said Mr Azim.

Mr Hope nodded. "I think that's enough to get on with."

Becky looked resigned, but Mum was still angry; anything that upset me or my helpers enraged her.

Sometimes she carried on fighting because she was a single mum used to fighting uphill battles all the time. Julian seemed indifferent.

I was delighted that Mr Azim had saved the meeting, without him, nothing would have happened. The bell rang again. The teachers left to start classes and Mum wheeled me out into the corridor which was empty again.

The following day, Mr Azim climbed the stairs at the end of Assembly. I was in the aisle near the back. Becky was beside me and beyond her were Jennifer and Emily. Mr Azim tapped the microphone which made my muscles tighten up.

"Most of you have seen or met Lauren Stark who joined Year Ten in September."

Lots of people turned round and looked at me.

"Lauren is a very special person - "

What did 'special' mean?

Special forces kill people behind enemy lines. Special schools warehouse people in wheelchairs and stunt their ambitions.

I was just ordinary; my life was strange and different to other people's but this is the way my life had always been. I felt embarrassed but pleased that Mr Azim had made the effort and I hoped that someone would volunteer.

" – every Thursday. All the details are on the notice board in the main entrance. The circle is open to anyone; you don't have to be in Lauren's class. As long as you can commit to coming every week then sign up but be quick; we only have space for ten people."

Everyone started filing out of the hall. Jennifer stood up.

"I'll come," she said.

"And I will as well," said Emily.

Thanks.

I was pleased.

"Will we get to drive your chair?" said Jennifer.

"You can drive Lauren to maths now if you like," said Becky.

"Okay," said Jennifer.

My class was due to start in five minutes. Becky showed Jennifer the joystick and the keys to press on the back of my chair. Jennifer turned the chair around.

"Make way," she said to the queue of people ahead. Anthony was right in front of us, telling Matt:

"I don't want to miss football, even if it's only one day a week."

So he wouldn't be coming. Shame. The chair lurched suddenly to the right and the footplate rammed into the back of Anthony's legs, causing him to fall backwards onto me. I didn't know who was more surprised, Anthony who landed gently in my lap or me.

"Ow, my leg," he said, rolling about on top of me which put my thighs into painful spasms but it stirred me up.

"Anthony, I'm terribly sorry - " said Jennifer.

Anthony turned round and looked straight at me. "Did you do that?" Then he started laughing.

"No, it was me," said Jennifer.

"Of course," said Anthony, "it wasn't you, Lauren, was it?"

"I'm helping out by taking Lauren to maths."

Jennifer scuttled round in front of me and leaned over more than she needed to help Anthony out of the chair.

I saw the colour of her polka dot bra so I'm sure Anthony did as well. Then Anthony overdid his 'dazed victim' act so Jennifer had to support him by the shoulder. They both giggled.

"Are you okay, Lauren?" said Becky.

Yes.

Having a boy land on me like that unexpectedly had shocked me but it wasn't all bad; Anthony had come close and spoken to me. He knelt down on one knee and lifted his trouser leg to examine the graze on his ankle. He looked like a little boy saying: 'look at my bad leg.' Jennifer played a suitably motherly role.

"Does it hurt?" she said.

"It's caning," said Anthony.

I wanted to vomit. Did I have to watch this boy-girl pantomime playing out right in front of me? It was Anthony I was angry with. He'd deliberately rolled around on my lap then played around with Jennifer. I felt stupidly jealous and I had a sneaking suspicion that was exactly what Anthony had intended. Boys.

By then the corridor beside the hall was empty. Jennifer drifted my chair towards the notice boards.

"There's Mr Azim's notice," she said, "no one's signed up yet."

"Come on," said Becky, "we're late. I'll take over."

"Fine," said Jennifer.

Anthony limped along behind us. Mr Todd had already started the lesson.

"You can have another go later, Jennifer," Becky whispered and she gave me a sly grin.

"Is that something we can all share?" said Mr Todd.

Mr Todd did slightly better in that first lesson after the crisis meeting. It wasn't his style that made it difficult to take in the equations it was Anthony, provocative irritating, Anthony.

Jennifer had a second go at driving my chair at the end of the school day. After watching the lovebirds in Assembly I had mixed feelings about her giving me a guided tour.

You won't drive me into the pond?

"What made you think that?" said Jennifer. "It'll be fun."

I trusted her. Becky called Jennifer's mobile and arranged to meet us at the entrance in twenty minutes' time. Jennifer led me down a maze of corridors. No surprise what she talked about.

"Anthony is so immature. I've known him since year five and he's never grown up. He's distractible; full of great ideas which never go anywhere. He hangs around with Matt who's a total science geek."

Anthony watches the girls very closely, I thought, especially you, Jennifer.

"I mean, when you look at him next to Dan who's shaving and whose voice broke months ago, there's no comparison."

I was pleased that Jennifer had chosen to bring me up-to-date on the subject that interested me most. There was some kind of axis between Anthony and me which felt dangerous and strong.

Was it hate, curiosity, attraction? I couldn't tell but I wanted to find out more. Five or six boys sat in front of computers in the library.

"Hello, I'm Miss Spake, the librarian," said a woman with curly black hair. "We're having a computer class but you can have a wander round."

We couldn't wander far. There were two steps up to the computers where the boys were so half the library was unreachable. The books looked old and there were lots of spaces on the shelves. A tattered copy of Terry Trueman's Stuck in Neutral was lying on the table. After a couple of tries, Jennifer succeeded in reversing out and we carried on along the corridor.

"I'll show you the Art Room and you can see some of Anthony's paintings. He's very artistic. He asked me to sit for him, fully clothed of course, but I refused; it didn't feel right. Then he complained that he'd have to stick to self portraits."

Over the years a lot must have gone on between Jennifer and Anthony. She fancied him, I could tell. Maybe she'd move on and talk about Dan or Matt or Jake.

"Ant can be a bit humourless sometimes; his Dad's a scientist."

As if that explained anything. The next window was too high for me to see into the classroom so Jennifer opened the door. There wasn't much to see, just maps and charts on the walls.

"Sometimes I wish he'd stop dreaming his life away and grow up."

She clicked into third gear down the long science corridor. Then she switched to fourth and I felt the wind blowing my hair. I felt safe despite Jennifer's accident in the morning.

"Wow, it goes fast."

We screamed to a halt when Mr Todd came out of a doorway ahead of us.

"I'm just learning to use Lauren's chair," said Jennifer.

"Sure," said Mr Todd, standing right up against the wall.

Jennifer pushed the chair through the double doors to the Assembly Hall and made a rapid circle with a full lock in the space below the stage.

"Are you okay?" she said.

I was laughing when we came to a halt.

There was a steep flight of steps up to the stage. How was I going to climb up to collect my prizes? We went back outside and Jennifer found Mr Azim's notice in the entrance hall.

"There's already three names on it," she said. "Emily, Liz and someone called Mary from Year Nine."

I knew it, all girls. Jennifer produced a pen from the inside pocket of her blazer and added her name. She took the chair outside into the quadrangle and changed down a gear to pass the pond.

"See," she said, "you're quite safe," she waggled the joystick, "quite safe."

The chair jiggled from side to side on the paving slabs right on the edge of the pond. I screamed but more out of excitement than fear. Jennifer's control of the chair seemed to have improved a lot since the morning. A long-tailed bird flew around me and landed on a water lily.

We went up a ramp into a corridor that smelt of pear drops. The Art Room had windows on two sides and a wall of shelves. Mr Azim was standing looking at the remaining wall which was crowded with sketches and paintings.

"Hello, Lauren and – "

"I'm Jennifer. I've signed up to join Lauren's group."

"Excellent, you're the first person to opt in."

"No I'm not, there's four names on the board now."

"Good, then it will definitely run. Were you happy about my announcement, Lauren?"

He looked at me as if he could read my thoughts but he couldn't. If my face expressed anything it was a mixture of embarrassment and delight. In just a week Mr Azim had become my favourite teacher.

"Do you paint, Lauren?"

Sometimes I can nod to questions but not this time.

"Don't worry," he said, "you'll make friends."

There were sculptures and ceramic bowls on the windowsill. Charcoal drawings, posters, pastel sketches and paintings overlapped each other up the wall.

"That's good," Jennifer pointed to a portrait in poster paints.

The girl in the painting had black shoulder length hair, she wore a bodice, her arms were raised and her eyes were half closed in a seductive pose. She was sitting in a wooden chair surrounded by wood as if she was from another age.

She could have been a gangster's moll or a sailor's dream of the woman he would meet.

Jennifer read the name clipped under the picture.

"Anthony Roberts," she said.

It was a portrait of me in the same position as the drawing in Anthony's maths book, with the same facial expression.

Mr Azim's gaze alternated between me and the picture.

"He's captured something," he said.

The girl in the picture looked like a hostage strapped to the chair.

"She looks like a doll," said Jennifer.

That was true. Mum told me once that I moved like Lady Penelope in Thunderbirds are Go. Did Anthony think I was a doll that he could dress and undress as he chose? Well I'm not; I've got a mind of my own.

"He did it in one afternoon," said Mr Azim, "apparently it's part of a series of characters that need saving in a computer game that he's working on."

I didn't know why we were all looking at it; it wasn't that good. I didn't like the idea of rescue. I didn't need a hero for a boyfriend.

"I'm hopeless at Art," said Jennifer. Her face and neck coloured.

"I wouldn't say that," said Mr Azim.

"I would," said Jennifer. "Look at the time, we need to get back."

We crossed the room and Mr Azim opened the doors for us.

"See you after half term, Lauren," he said as Jennifer accelerated through the Nature meadow and past a classroom with its rows of cookers.

"You're lucky. You don't have to do DT."

The next building was the gym where a yoga class was going on. Why couldn't I do PE? I'd have loved to see the fit boys exercising. I could wave my arms about. The trouble was I'd probably poke someone in the eye.

"This is where Anthony goes for Kung Fu," said Jennifer.

She was guessing what I wanted to hear, telling me what was on her mind. I liked that.

I couldn't quite imagine Anthony flipping opponents over with deft moves of his hips. I enjoyed my tour of the school and it had all started with Mr Azim's suggestion of a weekly get-together.

—

46

When we got home, Mum slammed the plates onto the worktop. What was it now?

I heard the phone beep several times through the evening as Mum made a series of calls. I could make out a few phrases: "exam", 'vulnerable" and 'disgrace". My heart began to pound.

Did she think that Anthony and I had sex already? I'd hardly spoken to him.

Anyway, wasn't I allowed to do what every other teenager does? Is someone going to stand over me like a judge and prevent me doing it?

It was a long time before Mum brought a tray upstairs. My mind was boiling over.

"Here you are," said Mum. She put the tray in front of me and picked up my hand and the board.

A disgrace?

"What? You've been listening in. It was a private conversation."

About me.

"I forgot about your hearing. Of course, when you want to, you can listen in to things miles away."

You were shouting.

"I'm sorry, Lauren, I'm not angry with you."

That upset me even more. Who was she angry with, Anthony?

"I had a letter from school about doctors."

I rocked in my chair and screamed. My arms flew about and knocked a full cup of juice onto the floor. Mum swore and left the room. Why is everyone trying to block me and set limits? Is she talking about a medical exam? What the hell is it to do with them?

Mum came back with a fresh drink ten minutes later.

"Lauren, you've got to be reasonable. I can't cope with you behaving like this."

I agreed to have a couple of spoons of beef stew because I was hungry.

"It's a summary of the crisis meeting we had. The head teacher has added a question about the use of FC in exams. He's asking me to give the names of professional people who support your use of the communication board. Where am I going to find them?"

I took a deep breath. I was glad Mum couldn't tell what I'd been thinking.

It might work out.

"How do you know?" said Mum.

Ryan manages fine.

My friend Ryan used FC and he'd had an invigilator all to himself for his exams. He was well on the way to university. Mum fed me the reheated stew and a slice of blackcurrant pie. I watched the lights come out over the city as the grey sky gradually change to night. Mum phoned up Ryan's Mum. Sheila, our neighbour, put me to bed. I stared at the ceiling.

I hoped Anthony would come over to talk to me again soon.

Mum was still clonking plates again the following afternoon.

"After all I've done," she said, "they're saying FC doesn't exist." She got the hoist twisted and thumped the controls.

It's not that bad. I can still go to school.

"That's not the point. It's the principle."

They can predict my grades.

"That might well be true. But anyone can see what a difference FC has made to your life. People say the facilitator has 'a major effect on the outcome'. Of course FC is going to be different with each person who does it. It's art, it's not science. They should know that."

―――

I felt the ground being cut away underneath me. I hadn't started off upset but Mum's anger started building up inside me. I wanted to swear. I needed someone my age to learn FC so I could let off steam.

Chapter 4

My group started in the Art Room underneath Anthony's painting of me. Six chairs made a circle round me: Becky, Jennifer, Emily and Liz, Mary and Mr Azim.

"Welcome to our first get-together," said Mr Azim. "A couple of ground rules: anything which people say here is confidential and be punctual; you need plenty of time to eat your lunch."

Mr Azim looked around the circle.

"Right," he said, "can you all give your names and say a bit about yourself? You start, Lauren."

I'm Lauren. I'm here because I want to meet people.

"I'm Becky, I've known Lauren for over a year now but I've been a note taker and personal assistant for longer than that."

"I'm Jennifer," she coughed, "I've come because I met you on your first day. I thought FC was cool and I knew straight away I wanted to be friends with you."

Emily's face went red and she hesitated before speaking. "You sit beside me in class – "

"Your name is – "

"Sorry, it's Emily. I'm amazed at how quickly you've caught up with the work."

"I'm Liz, I came because I like the idea of meeting up every week for a chat."

"Fair enough," said Mr Azim.

Mary had dark curly hair. "I'm M - "

"Can you speak up, please," said Mr Azim, "we can't hear."

Mary cleared her throat. She looked about to burst into tears.

"I'm Mary Munro, I came because my brother's got learning needs. He can't speak like you can, though."

I raised my arm so Mr Azim turned to me. "Lauren?"

Thank you, Mary. It means a lot that you've come.

It made me cry. Mary was so apologetic. It must have taken a lot of courage for her to join a group of total strangers from the year above. Becky dried my eyes with a tissue.

Mr Azim ran a hand through his slicked-back hair. "I'm Mr Azim and I'm here to learn. A school's just made up of people, people who can learn and I don't mean just the students."

I realised how tense I'd been when I noticed sweat running down my back when Becky sat me forwards. I was so pleased to find people who wanted to get to know me at school.

Mr Azim's lunchtimes became my favourite time of the week. People got emotional just talking about good or bad things that had happened. It wasn't all about me. Mary was upset when she came to the second meeting.

"I told you about my brother," she said. "You won't tell anyone, will you? He dominates our house, like we can't go to places because of him. I'd rather keep it secret. I want people to accept me as I am."

"I think we can all respect that," said Mr Azim.

Becky yawned.

"Sorry, I didn't sleep that well," she said.

"Maybe we should go outside," said Jennifer.

"When it's not raining," said Mr Azim, "we could."

You need a break, Becky.

Lots of good things came out of those meetings. I learnt about the lives of each person in the group. Jennifer had a younger sister that she often needed to look after when her Mum was at work. She was taking a grade six exam with the clarinet and it wasn't easy to practise. She was hoping to find people to play chamber music with. Jennifer asked me questions and let me choose between yes and no in response. She was starting to get answers.

Liz was madly in love with Jake but he liked to josh around with the boys. Emily was an only child who had a pet mouse that she released in her bedroom sometimes. She was incredibly sensitive to comments about her sight. She took her glasses off.

"I can read if the book is here," she put her hand an inch in front of her face, "but only one word at a time. My glasses distort everything. It's like looking through frosted glass."

I realised how hard she must work to get A's in English and that her silence when I first met was down to shyness.

Mary felt she had to make lots of sacrifices because of her brother. Her parents didn't give her enough attention. Mary, Jennifer, Emily and Liz all spoke to me if we met in the corridor.

Jennifer devised a rota to relieve Becky so that she could have a coffee and a cup cake in the school canteen when she finished working in the morning.

Jennifer sat with me outside when she was relieving Becky. That gave me a chance to watch the boys playing football on the sports field. Crows were calling from the conker trees whose leaves had all turned orange.

Anthony threw himself around like an angel in goal but he missed the ball which bounced through to where we were sitting. He came right up to us to collect it.

"Hi Jennifer," he said, looking all shy, "where's Becky?"

"She's having a break. I'm relieving her by sitting here with Lauren"

"Can I join you?"

"Aren't you in goal?" said Jennifer.

"It's someone else's turn now."

Anthony turned round and kicked the ball back. He sat down on the bench beside Jennifer. He was in his shirt sleeves and he was sweating. His elbows and the knees of his trousers were stained green from his diving. I could smell the crushed grass. He sat there for a while without speaking before he turned to me.

"Can I have a go at that FC thing?"

My mind went into overdrive. No, this is my chilling time, I wanted to say, but I couldn't. Anthony came round and picked the board from the right hand pocket of my chair. Stop it. I'd been enjoying just sitting and watching the wind in the trees. Anthony knelt down beside me and caught my hand which had flown up into the air.

"So you hold it like this?" he said.

It was outrageous. Leave me alone. He gripped my finger so that my index finger pointed towards the board. Then my arm moved.

****ing **** off.

Anthony looked stunned.

"No need to be like that," he said.

Perhaps he thought I didn't know those words. I was furious with him. How dare he just walk up to me like that?

"Sorree," he said.

"Did you just do FC?" said Jennifer, "just like that?"

"Yeah, kind of," he said.

"What did she say?" said Jennifer.

"She said 'Go away.'"

"Off you go then, buzz off," said Jennifer.

Anthony stood there for a moment before turning away and rejoining the footballers. My mind couldn't settle after that. I couldn't take in what had happened.

Normally when you like someone you keep meeting them at break times and when you're going in and out of classrooms but it wasn't like that with Anthony.

I knew he was avoiding me. Maybe he'd taken my words literally. Weeks passed without him saying a single word to me. He always missed the chance to work with me when the class was split into pairs. Emily and I were working on a primary source in history.

Our history classroom was gloomy because of the fog and because the science block overlooked it. There was one strip light that annoyed me by flickering on and off.

Anthony sneaked in late. He looked strange because his hair was sticking up. I had an irrational desire to put my arms round his long neck and cuddle up to him.

Emily said something.

Can you repeat the question?

"What's the matter, Lauren? I asked about Germany spreading the costs of the reparation."

Sorry, I'll have to read that passage again.

Emily laughed because she'd seen Matt come in and we both kept giggling for the rest of the lesson. Images of Anthony in his swimming trunks came into my head every time I tried to focus on the Weimar Republic.

Anthony and Matt came past our table at the end of the lesson. Becky still had the board out so I asked:

Anthony, did you see a ghost?

"What, I'm not with you?" he said.

"She means your hair," said Matt. "He dried it with the hand drier."

"Oh yeah," said Anthony, trying to smooth his hair down. "We had swimming. You have to do this." Anthony bent over so his hair stuck up even more. I could smell the chlorine.

"We had to dive down and pick up a brick from the deep end. You were useless," Matt told Anthony.

"Don't call me a spaz," he said. "I hate diving down."

Why bother if you hate it?

"I'm going for a badge," said Anthony, "the Bronze Medallion." He looked across the room at Dan who was chatting to Jennifer. "Dan's got his." Anthony left the classroom pressing his hair down but it wouldn't lie flat.

Next period, we were back in my favourite classroom, 10D, for English. Mr Preston set us an essay:

"'Why does the Creature behave as it does?' I want five hundred words."

More to the point, why does Anthony behave as he does? It was a complete mystery. I often saw him with a pen in his hand but he didn't take many notes; he was doodling most of the time. It was the Friday before half term; ten days looming without the slightest chance of seeing Anthony.

"Or you can choose: 'The limits of Science,'" said Mr Preston. "You must include quotes and page numbers from Mary Shelley's Frankenstein."

At last, something I could get my teeth into that will take my mind off boys. Anthony groaned along with Dan and Jake.

"Come on," said Mr Preston, "you should be able to recall the themes we've talked about: revenge, betrayal, alchemy, ambition."

Even I couldn't remember those. Anthony was bright but he lagged behind like most of the boys with 'C's and 'D's while Emily and I fought to get the most 'A's. Sometimes I thought that Anthony would be a bad influence on me if we did get together.

I heard him in the corridor, raving about a rock band which didn't interest me in the least.

But when I caught a trace of his aftershave I just wanted to be beside him whatever he was doing.

By lunchtime the fog had cleared. Jennifer, Emily and I took up our favourite position on the bench overlooking the playing field. I felt the autumn sun on my face while Becky spooned vegetable lasagne which tasted of roast tomatoes and olives into my mouth. Anthony was running around on the field a hundred yards away.

"I've brought the invites for my party," said Jennifer. She held up a stack of pink cards and read out the words:

Dear ....
Please come to my 15th Birthday Party,
The Golden Dragon Chinese Restaurant
6pm October 31st RSVP Jennifer O'Donnell
07869 111111

"I like the colour," said Becky.

"Thank you. Can you come, Lauren?"

I raised my arm.

"That's a yes," said Becky.

At last, I'd been longing to meet people out of school and this was my first invitation.

"Good," said Jennifer, "Mum's booked a table for ten people. There's us three and Sam."

"That's five," said Emily, "'cos Becky or Lauren's Mum will have to come as well."

"True," said Jennifer, "and Jake with Liz, and Dan."

"That's eight."

The invitations were getting decided before I could have my say. I was annoyed that I was being left out. Eating lunch takes me twice as long as everyone else.

"That leaves two spaces," said Jennifer, "I wondered about Abby and Carla."

I was almost gagging on the pasta.

"Just a minute," said Becky. She fitted a straw into a carton of blackcurrant juice and I drank it until it made a loud slurping sound.

Emily had said: "Fine, Abby and Carla, if that's who you want."

It wasn't fair. Jennifer had written the names on eight of the invitations before I'd had a chance to speak. It took ages for Becky to put the carton away, get the letterboard out and pick up my hand.

What about Anthony?

"Well," said Jennifer, "I don't know."

I was on the edge of my seat; surely he would want to come.

Anthony's funny.

"I know what you mean," said Jennifer, "he invited me to a gig."

"I know," said Emily.

I didn't. My heart sank.

"How come you know about it?" said Jennifer.

Emily's face turned red. "Matt told me," she said.

Jennifer exchanged looks with me. Emily was coming out of her shell; she'd started talking to boys, well, to Matt.

"Yeah, Bombus were playing," said Jennifer, "not my kind of thing, really. Anthony only asked me the day before. If I'd known sooner, I could have cancelled my music lesson. Someone probably dropped out at the last moment. I wasn't gong to be his second choice."

I made an involuntary sound. Why didn't he ask me? I knew access would be a problem and that I'd have to queue up outside and that Mum would have to come too and that it would be too noisy for me but I couldn't help feeling resentful that he'd asked Jennifer and not me. She would have accepted if he'd asked her a few days earlier.

"He got into trouble at Rock Bottom," said Emily.

"Why, what happened?"

"He tried to sell the extra ticket. The security man pushed him against the wall and accused of being a ticket tout."

"Poor Anthony," said Jennifer.

My heart was pounding. Did she mean that? Did she care about Anthony?

"If Anthony came then Matt could come too," said Emily. Jennifer looked at me significantly.

"Alright then." She wrote the names on the last two invites. "Will you deliver them, Em?"

"No way."

I will.

"Will she manage that alright?" Jennifer said to Becky, not to me. It was painful when my best friend patronised me like that but she got it right most of the time. I waited patiently for Jennifer to put the invites in my hand.

"Right," said Emily, "I'm gonna visit the shop."

That was code for: 'I'm meeting Matt somewhere out of sight.' Jennifer and I pretended we didn't know. I was pleased because Matt and Anthony were best friends. They came to school together and went round to each other's houses. The more Emily saw of Matt the more likely I was to have a chance of talking to Anthony. I was just so glad that Jennifer had turned down the Bombus gig. If she'd gone then Anthony and Jennifer would have been an item by now.

Becky packed up the lunch things, brushed the crumbs off my coat and switched on my chair. We set off onto the muddy grass which was still hard from the frost. Anthony was playing in goal on the far side of the field. The wheels started to skid in the mud where the frost had melted when we were halfway across. I dropped the invites. Becky stepped round to the front of the chair and picked them up. Then she noticed my blouse.

"Your top button's come undone," she said.

She reached forward to do it up but I wriggled out of the way. What would Anthony think if I managed to loosen all three buttons? Would he think I was a slapper? I didn't really care at that moment.

"Shall I do it up?"

No, it's fine.

"Lauren, you're mischievous, aren't you?"

Put my mobile number on Anthony's invite.

Becky got a pen out and wrote on the back of the invite.

And my email address.

She put the invite back in my hand, manoeuvred round the muddy patch and called across.

"Anthony."

Anthony turned away from the game and collected his blazer. I wondered what his Mum would say about the mud on his trousers. My chair made the twigs crack as it rocked its way under the horse chestnut trees and stopped just short of the slope. Becky got the board out.

I've got something for you.

He rested his hand on the chair and there was a crack and a spark.

"Ow," Anthony whipped his arm away and shook his hand.

"Sorry about that," said Becky, "the chair's got an electrical fault. It needs fixing."

He rubbed his upper arm. "It went right across here," he said, pointing to his shoulder and across the left side of his chest.

Poor Anthony, that's where your heart is.

Becky and I laughed.

"Are you making fun of me?"

You looked so serious.

I couldn't keep a straight face.

"Lauren's got an invite for you," said Becky.

He reached forward tentatively and touched my hand. I'd had my nails painted with a rainbow sheen. He didn't say anything. His hand closed around my fist while he read the invite.

"All-you-can-eat Chinese food?" he said, "that's cool."

I rocked from side to side in the chair which made my chest swing about. I watched Anthony through half-closed eyes; he couldn't take his eyes off me.

"Will you be coming?" said Becky.

"Definitely, Chinese is my favourite."

I was willing him to turn the card over but he didn't. My hand clamped onto his shoulders like an iron claw and pulled him towards me. Becky prised my fingers open one by one to release him.

"It's just a reflex," she said.

I felt angry at Becky, then happy and anxious in quick succession.

Anthony as coming to the party. But what if he spent all the time at the party with Jennifer? He just stared at me. Say something.

"Can I do the board?"

He was self-conscious with Becky being there.

Okay.

He knelt on the grass beside my chair. Becky put the board in his hand and stood behind me.

"Hold this finger in your right hand," Becky closed his hand around my index finger. His fingers were warm. I could smell his aftershave. "You need a chair really."

My arm shot up with anxiety and pointed to the pigeons that were cooing in the tree above us.

"Bring it down towards the board," said Becky.

"You're really strong, aren't you?" he said, clenching his teeth.

"You need to be firm," said Becky.

My arm suddenly gave way and my index finger landed hard on the board.

"'I'" he said, "did that hurt?"

No.

My finger darted down to the board again. "C," he said. I was so tense I thought I might swear. He moved my finger from side to side over the board like Becky did. "Should I be looking at your face?"

No, you'll make me feel self-conscious.

'A'- 'N'. I can - '"

He was so close that my hair was in his face. I hit the letters: h-e-k-p.

"'I can help?" he said.

Yes.

"That's amazing," said Becky.

I heard Jennifer cough in the background; she must be coming across to see what was going on. Sweat trickled down from my armpit. My finger hovered over the board.

"I can help – " said Ant.

I was grinding my teeth.

"What comes next?" My finger hit the board again.

"U, I can help you?'"

Yes.

"Oh my God, I did it."

It didn't make sense to me. I was sure Anthony fancied Jennifer more than me. I was annoyed that my finger had tapped out what he wanted to hear. It was half me and half Anthony speaking really. Anthony raised his fist like a tennis player.

He relaxed and my fingers raced around the board making it clearer. I spelt:

I like u.

Then Jennifer arrived. A chestnut fell out of the tree and bounced on the ground not far from me.

"What did she say?" she said.

"Lauren made a sentence," he said.

"Wow," said Jennifer, "you're good at doing FC."

"It was easy."

As if it was all down to him and nothing to do with me. He let go of my hand and gave the board back to Becky. But did you get what I said, Anthony? He'd switched his attention to Jennifer; I couldn't tell if he'd understood me.

"That was amazing," he said. "Thanks for the invite, Jennifer, I'm definitely coming."

"Good," she said and turned to me. "Can I have a go at FC?"

No.

"I think Lauren's tired now," said Becky, "perhaps on a different day."

Becky drove my chair back across the field. I was furious. I felt close to Anthony and suddenly so far away moments later. After his amazing breakthrough, he totally ignored me. Everyone did while they were all congratulating each other. What about me? Did you get my message, Anthony? Do you like me? I can't blow dandelion clocks to find out. You need to tell me.

Chapter 5

"You woke me up five times in the night," said Mum.

Give me a break. I appreciate Mum's help but three consecutive days together over half term and her voice was like a cheese grater. I got restless in the night because not enough was happening in the day. Mum lifted me and turned me over but after a while I was calling out again because my head was against the edge of the boxed-in bed.

'Am I going to be chained to you for the rest of my life?' I thought. Mum struggled to put my clothes on. She hadn't got over the school's letter.

"I can't do with this," she said and stormed downstairs leaving me with only one arm fitted into the sleeve of my blouse. Why can't you accept me as I am?

She came back upstairs after half an hour, finished dressing me and it was fine. We have these bust-ups sometimes. They flare up and vanish as quickly as they came. Carers need to let off steam, I know that.

I couldn't stop thinking about Jennifer's party at the end of the week. I'd finished my maths and my history.

I asked Mum to check my email but there weren't any messages from Anthony. Marian called up. Mum put the phone on loudspeaker and got the board out. I was always glad to speak to Marian, the woman who'd taught me how to do FC and enabled me to speak for the first time aged eight.

"Hi Lauren, how's it going?"

Fine in English and History.

"That sounds a bit guarded. You mean not so well in the other subjects?"

I'm not keen on my maths teacher.

"Yes, I heard about that. I had a suggestion."

"Yes, it's upset me a lot," said Mum.

"So why don't you call up Lauren's medical notes, Sarah, and track down a doctor who supports Lauren using FC?"

Mum rubbed her chin at that.

"What about science, Lauren?" said Marian.

Science is okay.

"Do you do any art?"

I paused.

No, I'd need a lot of help to manage that.

Mum butted in: "Would you like to come over for tea, Marian? Lauren's been a bit up and down recently. I'm sure she'd appreciate a longer chat."

"Sure, Sarah, I'll come over after work today."

Well done, Mum. Marian joined us at six in the big Victorian kitchen for tea and freshly baked cakes. I imagined it as it once was with a range and steaming pots and a super-efficient overweight cook and her assistants baking recipes from Mrs Beeton's cookbook. The view wasn't much, just the yard where the van was parked and the big house above us but the evening light filtered in through the large window.

Marian released her hair band and tossed her blond hair over her shoulders. Mum sat beside me with the board.

"It's been a long day, has it?" said Mum.

"It's not the students," said Marian, "it's their parents I can't cope with. They don't have the enthusiasm to make FC work. It's tragic when I see what a difference having a voice makes to the child. Then it's forgotten about or put away like some ornament in a cupboard."

You've got some pupils using FC.

"Yes, Lauren. That's what keeps me going."

And the research.

"Yes, which is on track. It's just I'm getting more referrals than I can cope with. Tell me what happened with your maths teacher."

Mum explained about the case conference and Mr Azim's get-togethers. Marian smiled. Mum's favourite soap was starting so she left Marian and me to chat on for a bit.

"So how are you and your Mum getting on?"

Dreadfully. This morning was the worst. Mum lost her temper.

Marian rattled off the FC. I could talk faster with her than with anyone else.

"I'm sure half term puts a big strain on you both," said Marian. "You get so absorbed in school and suddenly time stretches out in front of you."

She gets on my t*ts.

"Well you're growing up now, aren't you?"

That's it, I'm a woman now and she treats me like a child.

"You need take some time out with one of your helpers. What about making friends?"

Mr Azim's get-togethers are brilliant. I've got to know Jennifer and Emily who have lunch with me and Mary from the year below.

"Is that Mohammed Azim, by any chance?"

I think so. He teaches art.

"If it's the same person, I went out with him once," said Marian, blushing, "He's lovely."

The thought of Marian going out with any of my teachers was gross, especially a womaniser like Mr Azim.

Did you have sex?

"Now, Lauren, you know I can't answer questions like that," said Marian laughing.

She blushed so deeply I read the answer: 'Is the pope a catholic?'

"That's not polite. What about boys? You haven't said anything about them."

Anthony's done FC with me and he likes me but he's moody and he disappears for weeks at a time.

Slight exaggeration.

"And?" Marian guessed there was more to come.

He was rude about me at first.

"Maybe you've won him round," said Marian.

I'm not sure.

It was strange how talking about Anthony had drawn out something I hadn't consciously known. Anthony had a cruel streak and it hadn't gone away. It frightened me that my affection for him was growing. I could get hurt if he turned on me or ignored me.

"Men," said Marian quietly, "they're so much trouble."

Mum came back in and Marian had to go soon after that.

"Listen, Lauren," said Marian, "you're doing great. Don't work too hard and make sure you have fun. Bye, Sarah, see you both soon."

At ten o'clock Mum brought me through to my bedroom to hoist me into bed. She slipped the hoist sling underneath my bum and I brought my chair up against the bed that prevents me from falling onto the floor.

"I'll just check your inbox," she said.

She went into the study, tapped in my password and clicked on the messages.

"There's a message from Anthony," she said and she wheeled me into the study.

Suddenly my heart was on fire.

"'I love you, FC amazing, Anthony'," she read.

Oh my God, I didn't know that was how you felt about me. Anthony was amazing and so direct. I glowed all over. I had a vision of how different my life would be at the end of the school year. I'd have a regular boyfriend and he'd take me to the Widcombe Rising, a street party with singing and dancing. I didn't know if Anthony would be the boy who took me but he's the one who'd shown most interest so far.

But Mum punctured it all a moment later.

"Sorry, Lauren, I'm tired; I haven't got my glasses on, let me try again." She put her face right up to the screen. "'I love to do FC with you, amazing, Anthony.'"

Honestly Mum. Not the same at all. I had to read it myself to make sure I'd understood it.

Was he sending me a cryptic message and expecting me to rearrange the order of the words? No chance. He was just crowing over how good he was at FC.

Next day, Becky drove me out to a deer park to give Mum a break. We found the deer feeding among the oak trees. Becky led my chair over some tree roots to a bench where she sat down. The sun came out and everything that you could hear was natural.

"Where are the stags?" said Becky.

Exactly, just like school. Where were the boys? Where was Anthony? He was probably drooling over some heroine in a shot-'em-up console game. He hadn't been in touch since his one short email.

The deer came really close as they grazed on the close cut grass.

They didn't notice my chair because I was sitting down. I yawned which made a doe raise her head and suddenly they all took flight. Normally I'd be lost in the sounds of the wind in the trees and the rustle of the leaves. Instead of that I was listening intensely for the buzz of my mobile in the shoulder bag, not a peep. You ought to be here with me, Anthony.

On the day of Jennifer's party, my helper, Sylvia, washed my hair in the shower and dried it so it fluffed out nicely. She brought me through to my bedroom and gave me a board like an artist's palette so I could choose to the colours I wanted to wear.

My finger hovered over the blues before choosing the reds, a new pink push-up bra and a low-cut red cotton top and a port wine cardigan with slim jeans.

Will Anthony even notice?

Mum and I arrived at the Golden Dragon, late as usual. I joined Emily and Jennifer who were tucking into their starters. Twangy music was playing when Anthony and Matt came in through the doors. A waiter approached to take their coats but Anthony waved him away. He crept up behind Jennifer and tried to scare her by spreading his Dracula cape and showing his vampire teeth.

Jennifer didn't look at all pleased. Poor Anthony; everyone else was in T shirts and jeans. He went all embarrassed. He had to walk past a table of serious looking Chinese diners. He hung up the cape, spat out the teeth and sat down. I was mortified that he didn't come and ask Mum to move so he could sit next to me.

"They've probably never heard of Transylvania," he said.

Anthony went up to fill his plate with starters but he kept staring at Jennifer in her silver sequin dress and heels, wearing her birthday tiara. He was so transfixed that triangles of sesame toast fell off his plate and skimmed across the floor. It was like watching a disaster unfolding in slow motion.

Jennifer kept taking photos with her new camera. Dan managed to get in on most of them.

"Oh no," said Emily, looking at her phone.

"What are you 'oh my godding' about?" said Jennifer.

With all the noise and the music, I couldn't make out half of their words. Mum went to get some food.

Anthony finished his second plate, took a swig from his Fanta and came over and stood between Jennifer and Emily who were listening to music from my iPod. Anthony tapped Jennifer on the shoulder. She drew her breath in sharply.

"Hi, Anthony," she said, taking the earphone out. "What is it?"

"Can I take a picture?"

"We're just listening to music."

"I've got some live music on my phone," he said.

"Oh?"

"From the concert. Let me show you."

He clicked the buttons on his mobile until a picture came up.

"Here, it's wicked."

"Wow," said Emily, "is that Bombus?"

"Yeah," said Anthony, "live."

Jennifer glanced up briefly. "The sound's a bit scratchy," she said.

"I think it's cool," said Emily.

"You keep moving the camera," said Jennifer, "it's making me feel dizzy."

"They were great. I spoke to Ed."

"Ed, the drummer?" said Emily. "What did he say?"

"He signed his name a few times but when he got to me he said 'Sorry son, I haven't got the time'."

"Oh, Anthony," said Emily, "what a shame. Matt went as well, didn't he?"

"Yeah, what are you listening to?"

"We're not saying," said Jennifer, giggling.

Mum had gone to get some food so Anthony sat down next to me. To my amazement he pulled the letterboard out.

"Don't tell him, Lauren," said Jennifer, "you'll spoil it."

My head twisted away from him.

"Oop," I said. I was delighted but I might be too hyped up to do FC. Anthony picked up my hand which made my heart pump faster.

"Are you alright?"

Yes.

"What are they listening to? Is it rock music?"

No. S – p – a – n-

"Spandau Ballet?"

No.

Stop trying to guess.

C - a - n-'

"Can-can?" he said, "that can't be right."

Give me time.

Cantigas.

"Canti gas?" He said. "What's that? A band?"

"Doh," said Jennifer, "they're Iberian songs."

Anthony smiled inanely, not at me but at Jennifer.

"This is great," he said but he was still holding my hand.

Let's move.

"What?" he said. "Why, what's the matter? We're fine here."

Flashing lights.

"Where to?"

Evidently he didn't want to move.

Anywhere.

"What's going on with all this secret talking?" said Jennifer.

"Lauren doesn't like the bright flashes," said Anthony.

"Oh, I'm sorry," said Jennifer, "I didn't realise. It's good that Anthony can tell us."

"Shall I take you over the far side?" he said, pointing to the table across the room.

Yes please.

He switched on my chair and I swung from side to side as he drove it across the red and white tiles.

I was in heaven. Anthony spoke to me, the FC worked and we were together. The Chinese diners stared at me as Anthony bumped the chair clumsily into the legs of their chairs. Every step took us further from Jennifer.

Anthony moved my chair round so that it faced the fish tank. I could see Jennifer through the blue green water although the neon-coloured fish kept getting in the way. Flutey music was wavering up and down in the background. Dan moved in to whisper in Jennifer's ear. Anthony picked up my finger and held the board in front of me. At last we could talk.

F***ing c**t.

"What? What's the matter with you?"

———

You keep ignoring me.

"It is Jennifer's party."

Where were you at half term?

"What, did you expect me to text you?"

I thought you liked talking to me.

"I was practising my diving," he said.

What, every day?

"Are you winding me up?"

You dropped me like a stone.

"Matt and I went swimming. We've got the rescue initiative on Wednesday. It's the Bronze Medallion. They don't just give it to you."

He let go of my hand and turned to look at the fish swimming around. He noticed Dan joshing around with Jennifer.

"Shit. Anyway, what did you mean when you said you could help me?"

My arm reached up, grabbed hold of his hair and pulled him towards me.

"Hey."

I can't do these things to order; my body just takes over and they happen. Anthony's face impacted on my cleavage. It took half a minute for him to extract myself though I don't think he was trying very hard. We were camouflaged by the low lighting and the green water of the aquarium.

We weren't the only people enjoying ourselves. Matt and Emily had disappeared into a quiet corner as well. I was pleased I was wearing the red cotton top; I felt natural.

After a while Anthony sat up and rearranged his hair.

"You are hot," he said, "I can't lie." He wiped his mouth with a serviette. I was laughing. Anthony picked up the board which had fallen on the floor.

"What was that all about?"

Helping you.

"Oh, okay."

It was magical in the rippling green light of the fish tank with floaty music playing.

I felt as if we were underwater. Anthony had held my hand and I'd been able to say what I wanted. I was on the edge of a real conversation, a chance to share my fears and dreams.

Speak to me.

"There's nothing to say. I go to school, life goes on. What do you want me to say?"

I waited. Surely he could tell me more than that.

"Matt and I are writing a role playing game for the X-box."

At that moment I thought Matt was discovering something much more interesting with Emily. Poor Ant.

What are you feeling?

"That I'm being left behind," he said. His voice had changed; he was speaking from the heart. "Dan's so far ahead of me when it comes to chatting to girls."

You're doing fine with me.

He took a deep breath is as if to say: 'you don't count'. Then he looked around and the spell was broken.

"People are looking at us."

Who cares?

It annoyed me that Anthony had switched off suddenly and gone remote.

Mum always keeps an eye on me and Jennifer had looked across a few times but I was never going to escape from that; everyone notices me.

What are you scared of?

"Nothing. Listen, I'm going to get some meat. Do you want something?"

I'm fine. Mum'll be back soon. She'll feed me.

Anthony stood up, slinked over and filled a plate with rice and slices of beef while Dan was playfully kissing Jennifer's neck.

When Anthony sat back down he looked disgusted at the way I'd drooled down my cotton top. He picked up a tissue and held it against my chin but at the last moment, my head swung away.

"Don't worry," said a voice behind us which made us both jump. Mum had come over. "It's a reflex."

"I didn't see you there." He let go of my hand.

"You two seemed to be getting on so well. I got another plate."

Anthony tensed up as if he felt guilty.

"Anthony," said Mum, "I'm really glad Lauren's got someone of her own age to talk to."

Shut up Mum.

"Yes. Right. I'll go and get some dessert."

Mum brought me back to the table. Matt reappeared and I overheard Anthony telling him about showing the Bombus pictures to Jennifer: "But she didn't seem that fussed."

"Jennifer's not really into rock music," said Matt, "she plays the cello."

"How do you know?"

Oh, Anthony, wake up.

I replayed the events of the day while I was lying in bed. My movements stopped and started unpredictably all the time, I'm used to it. It infuriated Mum when I lost my swallow for no reason at all. She knew I wasn't sulking but it looked like that, I couldn't help it.

Something strange had happened by the fish tank. I just reached out and pulled Anthony close. It shocked me. I didn't know whether it was pheromones or desire but I wanted to feel that moment of freedom again. It wasn't a miracle cure or a dramatic recovery it was just that sometimes my body worked the way I wanted it to.

Anthony had responded to that moment and let himself talk openly to me. Then the wall came down. You never kissed me goodbye, Anthony. I was ready but you disappeared.

I felt hungry for more. I was curious to hear Anthony speaking from his heart. I began to be curious about his body underneath his T shirt. At least he spent most of the party with me. I knew I'd made an impression. I used to wonder how I would know if a boy fancied me. It was instinctive. I just knew, even if he didn't.

Chapter 6

How did Anthony get on?

I'd got Mum to phone Liz because she'd been doing the bronze medallion too. Mum took the phone off the cradle and brought it through into the lounge. It was a cold evening so she'd lit a fire in the grate that was crackling away. I'd been planning to stay on at school to watch Anthony's rescue attempt but his stonewalling annoyed me so much I decided not to bother. Anyway the chlorine would have affected my throat.

"It was awful," said Liz, "he's not a strong swimmer. He got hit on the head by Jake who was being the drowning casualty."

"Just a sec," said Mum as she sat down and picked up the board.

No, really?

"Yes, Mr Murphy let Anthony finish early."

Poor Anthony.

I felt as if water was filling my throat and filtering down onto my voice box at the same time as a blow to the side of my head. It was a strange feeling.

"He looked miserable."

Was he hurt badly?

"He said he was seeing stars but he was okay."

Do you think he passed?

There was a loud crack.

"I dunno. What was that noise?"

Just the fire.

"We have to wait a couple of days for the results."

What about you?

"I did alright, I think."

Fingers crossed, Liz. See you tomorrow.

"Bye, Lauren."

I couldn't get comfortable that night. My legs went tight and my body pressed itself against the wooden boards around my bed. Mum had to get up to shuffle my legs around. The pipes groaned and the blocked-up chimney whistled in the wind. It had a history, our house, with its servants' quarters in tiny attic bedrooms and my room, the old master bedroom. What secret liaisons might have been carried on via the servants' staircase which ran from the kitchen to the landing? What messages would have been transferred from the kitchen to the rooms upstairs by the dumb waiter?

I thought about Anthony's hopes for his video game; that it would get taken up by Sony. I wished he'd focus on things that were possible like doing better in exams. I felt guilty about not being at the pool but I couldn't have done anything.

Typically, Mum dropped me off at school just as the classes were starting so I had to sit through maths and French before I had a chance to talk to Anthony.

Julian cornered Anthony on the science corridor.

Let Anthony do the FC.

"Oh alright," said Julian. "I'm not needed apparently."

Anthony put his backpack down and knelt beside me.

Nasty bruise.

"I know," he said, rubbing the bump on the side of his head, "it hurts."

What happened?

"Jake practically knocked me out. I swallowed a lot of water."

Just like the sensation I'd had when Liz was on the phone.

I heard you practically drowned.

"Nah, it wasn't like that. It was just an accident, that's all. But it's caning."

Good Lick.

"What? Show me that again."

Good Luck.

"Thanks, your hair looks nice."

You like?

"Yes."

Then it was time to go into science. Good lick! Some of my mistakes with FC were too revealing. I was curious about the shape of Anthony's body.

He was fidgety, constantly doodling, gangly, clumsy but capable of creating the most delicate paintings.

He tried hard in football but he wasn't as sporting as I'd imagined my boyfriend would be. He looked like superman when he dived around in goal but he missed the ball.

You liked my hair, Anthony. That's one of the few nice things you've said to me. I felt the rhythm of your breathing while you were holding my hand. I could sense your excitement at doing FC. It's funny even when you get it wrong. But you annoy me by trying to guess what I'm going to say. I've been feeling upset about your rescue attempt. What's the point of that? I can't do anything about it.

We had to write a paragraph about one element in the Periodic Table. Julian wrote out my words:

'Antimony 51 exists as a shiny metal which looks like a cluster of silver spears pointing in all directions or a grey powder.

'Egyptians used one form, stibnite, as black eye shadow. Its alchemical symbol is a cross over a circle, the alchemist Paracelsus believed antimony cured many illnesses. It's poisonous when inhaled, drunk in water and on skin contact.'

Antimony was dangerous. Naturally when I thought of Antimony's two fold nature and its spiky structure I wasn't only thinking of semiconductors. I overheard Anthony talking to Matt when we were leaving the science class

"The Space Troupers are winning," he said, "annoyingly."

I picked up a lot of conversations that made no sense to me. I don't play computer games or watch TV. The conversation continued while I followed them along the corridor.

"I'm working on the essay," said Matt. "When science goes wrong, like when students volunteer for drug trials and end up in Intensive Care."

"Sounds complicated."

"Not really, and I'm writing about flesh-eating microbes that live in hospitals."

"Yuk."

"It's like Victor starting out with a grand idea which goes wrong."

"That's too complicated for me. I want to do something futuristic, like science fiction."

That set me thinking about Frankenstein's creature being in different places and times.

Becky couldn't get my chair close to the board when the lifesaving results came out. Team sheets for football and chess had been put up so lots of people were jostling each other to get near the board.

"I made it," said Matt.

Anthony jumped up, shaking his fists.

"Yay," he said, punching the air. "I did it. I got the Bronze Medallion."

"Alright, alright," said Jennifer, "Liz got hers too."

"Did she? You've had your hair cut."

"That was over a week ago, actually," said Jennifer. "How's the Kung Fu?"

"I've given it up for now," he said.

Anthony came over to me and picked up my hand.

"I actually did it," he said, "I passed."

As if I hadn't already heard. He didn't stay long.

"Where's Dan?" he said.

I almost wished he'd failed; he'd be more interesting to talk to. It was like he'd won the X Factor or something the way he boasted about it to all his friends. Am I just another trophy for you to show off? 'Look at me, I can do FC and no one else can.'

I feel left out.

"I do what I can," said Becky. Then she started to cry. Spare me. All that emotion gets channelled through me so I was doubly upset, once for me and once for Becky. She'd just split up with her boyfriend and I could feel her anger and deep sadness welling up at that moment.

Becky did what she could. She filled me in on the TV programmes everyone was watching. She got the board out as quickly as she could so I could join in, but things moved too fast. People would be talking about something else by the time I was ready to speak.

There will be better times.

I sat by the window in the dining room at home and watched the evening sky going a deeper blue. The wind made the rushes around the pond sway about. The yellow evening primroses and the red rose hips in the front garden gradually faded into black.

"What's up, Lauren?"

Anthony got his medal.

"Oh, that's good," said Mum.

He didn't say much to me.

"I'm sure he will if you give him time."

Easy to say that.

"Now, now, Lauren. Don't get nasty."

The girls hug each other and link arms and whisper about the boys.

I'm always on the outside.

"Jennifer talks to you."

She kneels down to talk to me.

She does 'yes and no.'

Anthony was the only boy who came anywhere near me, or used to. He'd vanished for a week after getting his precious medallion.

It was as if he couldn't bear to be seen with me. The two forms of antimony, I thought. He got worked up and his anxiety stayed with me as sharp spiky crystals. I had to block him out so I could get on with my school work. I didn't need this. I'm getting psyched up and I didn't even know why.

Next day, I overheard Anthony imitating our history teacher whose teeth overhang his chin. He was forever making fun of people. He was sweet when he noticed my hair but he'd been completely silent on the things that a girl wanted to know. What makes your heart sing, Anthony? Rock music and computer games?

—

Anthony was all cryptic and random while I was as straight as an arrow. He was a level ten geek, but he had a funny, tortured way of doing exactly the wrong thing that sometimes made me laugh but mostly annoyed me intensely.

He was vain and incompetent but he read better than angels did, if you could imagine angels reading Frankenstein. I wished I could help him chill.

Read your horoscope, Anthony: 'A dark force will undermine your resistance and you will find yourself well outside your comfort zone,' guaranteed. I've got a plan for you that's going to turn everything upside down, no mistake.

Emily, Jennifer and me and Becky sat around a table at lunch watching the boys come in. The canteen was a huge room with rows and rows of tables and a hatch with self service meals.

It was crowded because rain was pelting down outside.

Emily had reserved a couple of chairs for Matt and Anthony. Anthony came and sat opposite me.

"Did you finish your Frankenstein essay, Matt?" said Emily.

"It's lunch break," Anthony cut in, "can't we talk about something else?"

"It's due in this afternoon," said Matt. "Yeah, I did – "

"What, today?" said Anthony, "I haven't started mine yet. What did you do?"

"The Limits of Science," said Matt, "when discoveries go wrong and do the opposite of what they're supposed to."

"Plenty of scope there," said Emily.

There's lots of places where science can't go.

"Like where?" said Anthony.

"Love, for instance. Science can't explain that."

"I'm not writing a gay essay about love," he said.

"Actually," said Matt, "scientists have investigated the hormones that are released when two people meet."

That doesn't explain it.

"It will," said Anthony. He and Matt were ganging up on me.

What about emotions?

"You can measure them," said Matt. "Scales measure how happy you are and that kind of thing."

They're not accurate. They can't be. Scientists can't tell what you're thinking.

"They might," said Anthony.

"Actually they can," said Matt. "Functional imagery of the brain shows which areas are activated –'

Oh, I'm not arguing with you two. You're not listening to me.

It was silly of me to expect boys to talk about romance of course. But I felt upset by Anthony's put-downs and Matt's so-called science that explained absolutely nothing. Anthony and I were incompatible. He'd been blinded by pseudo-science and computer games.

"None of this is going to help me get my essay done," said Anthony. "I'm not going to write about clever science or "Lurve'. What did you do, Lauren?"

About how tragedy results when men ignore women.

Jennifer thought that was hilarious.

"Really?" she said, "that sounds perfect."

Anthony didn't say a word except:

"Have you got any other ideas, Lauren?"

Yes. Bring the creature up to the present.

"Like if it played football with us?" said Anthony.

Exactly.

Anthony paused as if a light had gone on inside his head.

"Go on," he said.

I thought: 'I'm not going to write it for you.'

He wouldn't read books, would he?

There was silence for a moment and Jennifer looked from me to Anthony.

"No, he'd play computer games and watch DVD's," he said. "You mean I could write about that?"

Why not?

You're supposed to be able to weave anything into an essay.

Anthony went thoughtful and looked up at the ceiling. I'd actually got through to him, with all these people around the table and all this clamour in the room. It was so tantalising. Most of the time Anthony was completely absorbed in his little world of gadgets and games and once in a while he stepped out of it and actually listened.

A week later, I grabbed hold of Anthony's blazer and pulled. It was the end of the last lesson. He was trying to squeeze past my chair to give in his English essay.

"Oi."

Becky leapt up to catch Anthony as he overbalanced.

"I think she wants to talk to you," she said.

I'm not 'she'. Anthony dropped his exercise book onto Mr Preston's desk. Becky stood up:

"Anthony, I've got some books to take back to the library," she said. "If you'd like to take Lauren to the reception area I'll meet you there."

She got my scarf and mittens out of the backpack.

"I can do that," he said.

Becky glared at me, meaning: 'you minx.' I hadn't exactly planned it. It was just sensible. If Becky had taken me with her I'd be left on my own while she queued up at library. It was the end of a long day and I was pleased I'd caught Anthony's attention and that Becky cottoned on to what I wanted.

"She needs her coat on as well."

Anthony would be putting all my outdoor clothes on.

"I'll see you in five minutes," she must have seen my face, "alright, ten minutes."

Anthony wheeled me round to the reception area. He wrapped the scarf round my neck and slid his hand inside my blazer to tuck the ends in. It was heavenly. He was very gentle. I helped him lean me forwards so that he could fit my right arm into my coat.

It's always a struggle when my arm tightens up at a right angle. Anthony found it impossible. Mr Preston happened to be passing by. He stopped beside me and put his case down.

"Let me help with that," he said.

No, don't. Let Anthony struggle on his own; he was doing fine. Mr Preston lifted me forwards and Anthony threaded my arm into the other sleeve. "I'm glad that you two are getting on so well," said Mr Preston. He stood up, picked up his case and went into the Staff Room.

"Shall we wait here?" said Anthony.

No, I need some fresh air.

School had been stuffy all afternoon.

Anthony actually held my hand as he guided the chair through the doors and down the ramp.

The fog made it seem like night time. I enjoyed the cool feeling of the air in my throat.

Anthony parked my chair under the corrugated roof of the bike shelter. Every so often drops of water fell from the roof onto my head. Anthony got the board out, knelt on the concrete floor and caught hold of my arm which was waving in the air.

The creature comes to life.

"Don't talk like that," said Anthony, "you're frightening me." He looked pale from the cold.

Where's your coat?

"I never bother with it," he said, "it's just more to carry round."

How's your head?

"Fine. I still can't believe I got the medallion."

I was enjoying the warmth of his hand in mine. But the conversation faltered. It's supposed to be easy talking to someone who likes you.

What are you doing tonight?

"I'm going round to Matt's. We're designing this game - "

He went on about levels and characters. I couldn't be bothered to listen.

What about Kung Fu?

He stood up to demonstrate some Kung Fu moves complete with the swishing sound effects. I don't think he'd noticed the people laughing as they went by.

Why did you stop going?

"Because I kept getting thrown by fat girls who were younger than me."

I had mixed feelings about Anthony flying through the air in white pyjamas and landing painfully. I wouldn't want young girls putting their hands all over him but I was curious to know how he'd react.

I'm angry with you.
"What? What have I done now?"
You've been avoiding me.
"Is that what I'm doing now?"
No, but I won't see you for weeks now.
"You know I like doing FC."
Yes, but what do you feel about me? Boys are much happier talking about things than people.
You never volunteer to work with me.
Which might be a good thing because we wouldn't get much work done. Anthony prompted me to speak again but I signalled 'no'. We were going round in circles. I watched my breath condensing in front of my face. The fog got deeper and Anthony held onto my hand. He leaned across and whispered:
"Can I put my hand inside your blouse?"
Yes.
I wasn't expecting his hand to be so cold. My legs kicked out which made me slide down the chair. My pelvis got trapped between the restraining belt and the seat. The pommel of the chair pressed into my crotch. I screamed out in pain.
Lots of people must have heard me, there were loads of people coming out of school. Anthony panicked. With one hand down my back he grabbed hold of the crotch of my trousers and tried to hoick me up the chair. It was a bit clumsy but I was more comfortable in the end.
A woman I didn't know came right up to me.
"Are you alright, Lauren?"
Complete strangers knew my name.
"Yeah, she's fine," said Anthony.
I'd been enjoying the human contact but suddenly I felt embarrassed and confused.

I didn't like the way Anthony answered for me.

"What's been going on?" said Becky when she joined us. Anthony hadn't bothered to brush the hair out of my eyes and my clothes looked dishevelled.

"Nothing," said Anthony, letting go of my hand.

Mum appeared. Anthony stood back and Becky did the FC.

I just slid down the chair and Anthony helped me.

"Thanks, Anthony," said Mum.

Anthony disappeared into the fog without saying goodbye. Mum took me to the Rainbow Café. I didn't like going anywhere in school uniform but it made a change from going straight home.

As Mum brought me into the warm café, I smelt the roast peppers, garlic, jacket potatoes and fresh ground coffee from the kitchen behind the counter. We sat at a table against the wall.

"I think I'll have the orange and pumpkin soup," said Mum. I chose a chocolate milkshake.

A group of businessmen at the next table were talking about balance equations. Anthony had told me he didn't like talking on Facebook because there was always someone else there.

I can't share things spontaneously like my friends do. I don't want to think about how hard some things are just when I'm starting to feel I belong in school. It's great having friends. I missed that all the time I had a home tutor.

I want Anthony to come here during the holidays.

"Would he come, do you think?"

I don't know. He was very shy. Until we had sex last week.

"Ha, ha, Lauren, I think you're winding me up. I hope so. I can probably find something to do, like some shopping and leave you two on your own. Is that what you'd like?"

I'll be fine, Mum. Who knows what might happen?

"I know, that's what worries me."

I can't cope with Mum's angst about boys. Leave it to me.

What's it like to have sex?

"Not this question again, Lauren. You'll have to ask someone else. It's been so long I've forgotten all about it."

That's no help.

Chapter 7

Towards the end of assembly, Anthony joined Jake and Liz at the foot of the stairs while Mr Murphy, the swimming instructor addressed us all.

"The Lifesavers' bronze medallion," he said and read out the names.

Jake and Liz collected their medals.

"Anthony Roberts."

Anthony climbed the steps collected his medallion and I felt warm all over. Go on, show people what you can do. He turned to the audience, lifted the badge into the air and smiled broadly. The applause practically died out and Anthony turned and almost tripped over going down the steps.

I saw Anthony strolling around the corridors showing off the badge to everyone. At lunchtime he actually approached me in the quad.

"What have you been telling Jennifer about the bronze medallion?"

The truth.

"Oh yeah, like I nearly drowned?"

"I'll leave you to it," said Julian, handing the board to Anthony. "Call me when you've finished."

Anthony hung his blazer on my chair and sat down on the bench beside me which faced the pond in the centre of the quad.

"There's no need to go round insulting me."

You got the badge. Can't you see the funny side?

"No, actually I can't."

Our first real argument.

"You make it sound as if I haven't earned it."

No, I didn't.

"I put myself out to help you. I learnt FC and all you do is put me down."

F*** off, Anthony.

If you want someone to rescue, I thought, find someone else. I'm not a charity case. I can cope perfectly well on my own. Anthony threw the board down and left. He had no idea how that left me stewing all afternoon. It really matters to me how people leave me. I was furious.

Julian came home with me that night because Mum was going out to a musical event. He put my chair in the dining room and set about making tea. Radio 3 drifted through the hatch.

I began to feel I'd been mean to Anthony and I ought to find some way to make up. So after tea I asked Julian to take me upstairs so I could go on the internet. Julian wheeled my chair into the lift, shut the door and activated the lift. I floated vertically up through the ceiling and into the study.

Meanwhile Julian ran up two flights of stairs and tried to reach the button to open the lift door before I'd reached the top.

It was one of the games he regularly played and he didn't often make it in time. Sometimes I wondered if he dawdled on the stairs to make it seem more exciting.

He opened the lift door and wheeled me up to the computer. Julian clicked a switch and the big screen came to life.

"Did you want to do research on something?"

No, I want to send an email.

He brought up my email inbox.

New message to Anthony Roberts.

I watched the cursor flashing in the message field.

Sorry about today. Would you like to meet me at the Rainbow Café on Tuesday afternoon? Come at 3.30 x Lauren.

Anthony accepted me as a friend on Facebook on the following day.
He must have looked at the pictures of me with Mum and Becky by the sea and on a boat and of my toy dog. Becky read out Anthony's reply.
Okay, see you on Tuesday.

The weekend passed slowly while I was thinking about meeting Anthony. I kept thinking about what clothes I might wear and what we might talk about. I finished my homework early.
Jennifer came round and Mum and I made a team and played Scrabble against her. I made up 'KISS,' 'LOVE' and 'ANT.'
"It's pretty clear what's on your mind," said Jennifer.

On the Tuesday, Mum guided my chair into the Rainbow Café. "I'm not in love," was playing and I immediately felt excited. I was wearing my red polo neck sweater and Fuchsia pink cardigan and blue jeans. I made an impression because the girl behind the counter smiled and waved at me. There was no sign of Anthony but we were twenty minutes early.
We waited, the clock ticked round slowly.
"I can't live," sang the loudspeakers. I tried not to listen to the songs but they all seemed to be about unrequited love. As time dragged slowly on I felt as if someone was deliberately torturing me with songs about betrayal. Mum lifted my hand at twenty past three.
He's not coming.

"Horrible little boy," she said.

When we got home I asked Mum to wheel me to the summerhouse.

"It's dark," she said.

I started to cry.

"What was he thinking of?" said Mum.

I invited him to come to my favourite place.

"And he didn't come."

Mum went off to make tea. Have you any idea how that feels when you've had your hair done? My life is so public. When things go wrong everyone sees it. I'm never going to speak you again, Anthony. There was a rustling behind the summerhouse. I told myself it was a blackbird and not a rat.

Aren't I good enough? Don't I deserve respect? Why did I even think of inviting you? I don't need a pathetic loser. I've had a lot to put up with in my life and I don't need someone who's going to wobble and be unreliable. You might make a good friend to someone else but not me. That's it.

I didn't believe in telepathy so I didn't feel any better when I let my anger run on. No one could hear me. Mum brought me indoors and used the hoist to give me a bath but it didn't wash away my angry thoughts.

It wasn't good for me, going to this cold place but what could I do?

"I'm furious with Anthony for not turning up," said Mum.

Stop it. You're probably just angry at Dad who left us after I was born. Let me sort myself out. I watched the rain landing on the window, well wrapped up in my chair.

The ash tree made a sound like a waterfall in the wind while the apple tree stood still and silent with its arched canopy like a huge umbrella. Anthony let me down but I wasn't going to let that spoil everything. I listened to the rain falling on the leaves and the jackdaws calling.

I came in at seven. Mum brought a tray with hot chocolate and cup of tea for herself.

Can you call Jennifer on the landline?

Mum balanced the phone of the table and got the letter board out so that I could talk to her.

"Hi Jennifer, it's Sarah here, Lauren's Mum. Lauren wants a word."

"Hi, Lauren, what's up?"

I'm upset.

"Oh, why, what's happened?"

You know I was meeting Anthony at the café –

"Oh no, don't tell me – '

He didn't come.

"What a shit. I don't believe it. I'll get him for this. He's such a creep."

I haven't decided what to do yet.

"Just forget about him, that's what I'd do. I'm calling him but he's turned his mobile off. I'll send a text, that'll put him in his place."

I'm not asking you to do that. I'd rather sort my own life out.

"Too late, I've done it now."

I've got to go now.

"Wait, Lauren. Can we meet up tomorrow and go round the shops?"

Yes.

I'd answered without thinking.

"I'll ask Em if she can come too. Would twelve o'clock suit you?

Yes. Bye, see you tomorrow.

"Bye, Lauren and don't be upset over Anthony, he's not worth it."

Anthony's email about not coming was the first message in my inbox.

Delete, what's next?

I've had some tough things happen to me. Anthony had no idea. I started reliving the nightmare events of my life, starting with being born and not being able to breathe, then when I was in hospital for an operation aged seven, hearing the nurse say:

"You should never have been born."

The darkness closed around me and fingers clutched at my throat. I wasn't sure if any of this had ever happened, it seemed like a scene from a film but it scared me all the same.

Mum tried frantically to feed me beef lasagne. It just wouldn't happen.

My head turned away, my jaws remained resolutely closed and my throat would not swallow any food that reached my mouth.

"Come on, Lo," said Mum with increasing desperation but it made no difference. "I'll try again later. Is it that boy?"

It wasn't just Anthony. It was everything: the slow progress making friends, Mr Todd questioning my work. Rejection concentrated at the back of my mouth. But my swallow could go for no reason at all. Just forget about him, that's what Jennifer had said. Anthony was the first boy who had taken the trouble to start learning FC. He behaved like a loser and he had no idea who he was. He was like a half finished painting. He needed the help to see that. That's what I could provide: a few searching questions that would shock him into life. I need people around me to be calm and supportive. Live with it. I do. Mum got the letterboard out.

Read me the paper.

"Grace is coming next weekend," said Mum, "that should cheer you up."

Mum read the financial news in a monotonous voice. It was the best way to let sleep come when my mind wouldn't stop going over things.

"Poor Lauren," said Mum, "you'll enjoy shopping with your friends tomorrow."

Was I wallowing in self-pity? I wasn't sure.

Can you put Purcell on?

"Which one?" she said.

Any.

Mum chose the opera: Dido and Aeneas.

I closed my eyes and listened until my favourite aria came on: Fear no danger to ensue. Then I fell asleep.

Chapter 8

I woke up tired and I didn't feel like going shopping. What was there to buy? On the other hand it was my first outing with my two best friends. Maybe I could treat myself to something special and then I'd feel better.

Jennifer and Emily were waiting for us when Mum parked up by the tram stop. A gale was blowing and the shelter had no sides so there was no protection form the wind.

'Clang.'

The tram arrived soon after. It was easy to get on; more like a ferry than the bus or a train.

We went first to the shopping centre and worked our way along the accessory shops. At each entrance Jennifer asked me:

"Shall we go in here?"

Yes.

'Yes and no' was easier than spelling out words with FC, pointing to the right for 'yes' and left for 'no'. It was quick but also frustratingly limited and sometimes my finger said 'yes' when I had meant to say 'no'.

Jennifer stopped at various places round the shop: the velvet scarves and the chunky jewellery. She chose a green dress for herself, some matching shoes and tights and Emily found a blue blouse. The bags were stacking up on the back of my chair but I hadn't bought anything.

"Do you like this?"

Yes.

Do you want to get it?"

Yes.

"I'll get your purse."

No.

It took a lot of time and Jennifer was getting frustrated.

"Let's get a drink," said Emily.

Jennifer and Emily bought drinks and we sat down at a table in the food court. Jennifer sipped her Red Bull with one hand and asked me yes and no questions with the other. It should have been the highlight of the holiday, a trip out with friends but I was upset about what had happened at the café. Emily sat opposite me.

"You're still thinking about Anthony, aren't you?" said Jennifer.

Yes.

I can't think about anything else: about why he did that to me and what he was feeling.

"You must be really annoyed with him?"

Yes.

"I can't believe what Anthony did," said Jennifer, "to say he was coming and then not turn up, that's unforgivable."

"Err," Emily had half-raised her energy drink to her lips but she put the bottle down.

"What is it?" said Jennifer. "You know something, don't you?

I turned my head towards Emily.

"Yes," said Emily, "Matt said that Anthony had to go to the dentist."

That was news to me. His email didn't say anything about that.

"So why didn't he send a text?" said Jennifer.

"I don't know," said Emily, "Matt didn't say. He just said that Anthony had lost a filling and he had to get it fixed straightaway."

I was amazed that Emily hadn't told me this before. It made me want to hear Anthony give his own explanation. Did something happen or was it just an excuse?

"It makes no difference," said Jennifer, "if someone did that to me I'd never speak to them again."

That's fine for you, I thought, but Anthony and I had shared something special at the Chinese restaurant. It made me cry to remember how quick he was with his first try at FC. I couldn't believe it was all over.

"Never again," said Jennifer.

I wasn't sure about her sincerity. Even though she was slagging off Anthony I knew she still had a soft spot for him. We set off again. Jennifer drove my chair into another clothes shop.

"Excuse me," said a shop assistant behind us. She was holding up a dress that had been knocked onto the floor as we went by. "This costs over a hundred pounds."

"I didn't do it deliberately," said Jennifer. "You've only left a narrow space between the rows."

I wanted to leave the shop straight away and find clothes somewhere else but Jennifer lingered around looking at coloured tights.

"You drive the chair for a bit," she said to Emily.

We went out into the open air, across the street and down the pedestrianised main street.

We made slow progress through the crowds with road sweepers and Big Issue sellers to work our way round. We passed a couple of charity shops before Jennifer stopped to speak to me.

"Carry on?"

No.

Five questions later she got it.

"The Oxfam shop?"

Yes.

It had been done up and Mum and I had seen some great clothes in lovely materials. It was Emily who found the rail of cast-off theatre clothes. She picked out a white silk peasant blouse and a black tie-up corset.

"What do think of these?" she said.

Jennifer picked up my hand.

Yes.

"No," said Jennifer, "when are you ever going to have a chance to wear those?"

Yes.

It was all I could say. Emily got my purse out and paid for them both. I'd got something I liked even if Jennifer thought it was a complete waste of money. I needed something different.

Jennifer insisted on visiting different sections of the big department store. The assistant bumped a clothes rail making the metal hangers clash together. The sound echoed in my eardrums and made my elbows go up.

"Sorry," said the assistant, "I didn't mean to do that. I'm Anne. Do you need any help?"

"We're looking for a hairband," said Jennifer.

"Let me show you." Anne led the way to the back of the shop and showed us all the different colours.

Jennifer got increasingly frustrated.

"There's nothing here," she said loudly.

The assistant moved the bargain rail out of the way for us.

"Helpful aren't they," said Jennifer sarcastically, "and clumsy?"

Personally, I thought Anne, the shop assistant, couldn't have done more to help.

Outside, it had started to rain. Emily led the way up the hill towards the tram stop.

"Lauren."

Someone called my name from the opposite side of the street, a girl's voice. A girl that I'd seen vaguely in the distance at school came towards us across the tram tracks.

"Jennifer," she said, "I'm glad I found you."

"Oh, Vicky," Jennifer sounded surprised.

"Anthony's here," she said.

I hadn't realised; she was Anthony's sister.

It was obvious when you knew. She's got the same high cheekbones. The pavement was narrowed with road works and my chair was practically blocking the way. Shoppers were rushing past us to get to out of the rain.

Anthony stepped over the tracks with a shy smile.

What's so funny? He was wearing his bleached jeans and just a T shirt.

"You?" said Emily.

"I've got something for Lauren," he said. The rain started pelting down. Anthony stepped onto the pavement and retreated under his sister's pink umbrella.

"It's too wet," said Jennifer, spreading her elbows out. "We're getting out of the rain."

Jennifer sped my chair up the hill, waited for a bus to stop at the pedestrian crossing and took me into the foyer of the corner house. It was like a cathedral except the walls were made of glass and two escalators rumbled away in the middle of the floor. We seemed to have stopped directly under the spotlights and the waiting shoppers made a circle around us that reminded me of a nativity scene.

"Phew, that's better," said Jennifer.

Some people were shaking their umbrellas and waiting for the rain to clear while others were choosing what film to see. Anthony and his sister joined us.

"Haven't you caused her enough trouble?" said Jennifer. "Now buzz off."

Vicky stood beside Anthony. She wasn't going anywhere.

"Is this some kind of nasty trick?" said Jennifer. "She won't speak to you."

"Alright then," said Anthony "will you give her this?"

He handed her an envelope. "Tell her I'd like to do FC with her and I've got something else to show her."

Why does everyone talk as if I'm not here?

"You are in big trouble and don't forget it," said Jennifer and she turned to me. "Do you want to look at this?"

Yes.

"Are you sure? It's from that scumbag Anthony Robot."

Yes.

I hate having to repeat myself. It was farcical. We were suddenly inside this tall building and it was like a court case with Anthony and Vicky on one side and Jennifer the prosecutor on the other. Two women in raincoats put their bags down and listened to Jennifer while they waited for the rain to stop. She held up exhibit number one, an envelope.

"'To Lauren,'" she read out. Then she tore the card open.

It was pink card with a green meadow and a bumblebee flying in a dotted circle around a purple flower. She opened it and read the text inside.

"'I'm sorry, Lauren. I didn't mean to hurt your feelings and I'll never do that again. I promise. xx Love Anthony.'" Jennifer paused. "Do you like the card?"

Those two x's meant the world to me.

Yes.

Jennifer turned to the bag that Anthony was holding.

"What have you brought, Anthony?" she said.

Anthony opened the shopping bag, took out a pink parcel and stepped awkwardly across the floor towards me. He had to bend down and put the parcel on my lap then he went back to his sister's side.

A lady with two shopping bags said "Aww."

Jennifer read out the label: "To Lauren, Love from Anthony. Do you want to open it now?"

Yes.

Jennifer tore the paper. "It's nice paper," she said. She opened it out and the sound made my hands go up in the air.

"Ah," I said.

Inside was a box that Jennifer opened out. It was a necklace with a silver Celtic knot and a purple stone. It sparkled in the shop lights.

"Oh, that is nice," said Jennifer, lifting the chain. She took off my red scarf and put the necklace over my head. The silver knot rested on my upper chest.

Anthony was hopping from one foot to the other. Jennifer put a make-up mirror in front of me so I could see myself. I smiled. My right arm lifted up.

"Where are you hiding, Anthony?" said Jennifer. "Lauren wants to speak to you."

Anthony crossed the circular space and knelt by my chair. Emily and Jennifer joined the circle of onlookers.

Think.

"What?"

Mistake. Thanks. I like the necklace.

Anthony read out my words. Lots of people were listening. It wasn't very grammatical. The silver knot shimmered on the edge of my vision.

You chose it?

"Did I choose it? Yeah," he said, looking at his sister.

Thought-

"Thoughtful?"

No. Thought so.

Stop jumping ahead. Give me time.

"I'm pleased you like it."

Kiss me.

Anthony didn't read those words aloud.

Now.

He patted my shoulder and stood up, still holding my hand

Coward.

The rain had stopped. People were shaking their umbrellas but lingering in the foyer to watch me and Anthony. A tear ran down my cheek as I looked around.

"What's the matter?"

I wanted to kill you. You were so cold –

My words flowed easily; I was angry.

I still want to know what happened.

"Oh, Lauren," he said. "Your eyes have a lovely pattern."

All the better to see you with.

"Aw, sweet," said Emily, overhearing Anthony repeating my words. He tried to shuffle away but I was pulling him closer. He extricated himself.

"Look, I will talk again soon, okay?" Then he joined Vicky and they went outside.

"It seems like you two've made up," said Emily when we reached the tram stop. "I'll call your Mum and let her know we're coming."

"You got a necklace?" said Mum. She'd taken me upstairs in the through floor lift. I was ready to go to bed but I'd have to wait until Sylvia came.

It was a present.

"What, from Jennifer?"

No, Anthony.

"Oh," Mum clamped her lips tightly shut.

To say sorry.

I sat in the bay window and watched the shadows shift across the garden. A robin landed on the lawn, searching for food. A crow dropped out of the apple tree and the robin vanished into the undergrowth.

I thought about Anthony and his role-playing war games. Was this the strategy he used: advance, withdraw, advance, withdraw, for ever and ever.

Each time we made a breakthrough like doing FC he'd vanish for a week. I'd see him in the distance but he wouldn't come anywhere near me. Maybe we'd never get any closer.

The crow flew away and the robin flew down onto the lawn again.

Chapter 9

It snowed. All my friends were overjoyed. Buses got stranded and school was closed for the first two days of the new term. I stayed in but Jennifer rang me to tell me she'd been snowboarding and making snow people and having snowball fights. It didn't cheer me up.

"Let's go out," said Mum. "You look miserable. Is it that boy again?"

No.

It probably was. I hadn't spoken to Anthony since he'd given me the present. I wore the necklace and I loved it but I couldn't forget the way he'd let me down. Mum took me shopping. The sloping pavement in front of the Law Courts had turned into an ice rink. My chair slid towards a bus that was already skidding across the road. It terrified me and I couldn't tell you about it, Anthony.

School started on Thursday, my favourite day of the week. At the end of English, Mr Preston called out:

"If you can bring your copies of Frankenstein to the front; we've finished that now. Tomorrow we'll start on A Midsummer Night's Dream."

People crowded around my table to give their books back.

"Yay," said Anthony, "a play."

"At least it's something different," said Matt.

I overheard Jennifer talking to Anthony. "Emily and I went to Rock Bottom last Saturday," she said.

He cleared his throat. "Did you?"

"Yes, it was the teen night."

"Was it good?"

"Yeah, they had some great bands. You two should come along next month."

"What? Matt as well?"

"Yeah, why not?"

Jennifer and Emily left the classroom giggling. I was being left out, as always. I couldn't compete with Jennifer. Becky walked me out into the corridor and got out the board.

Get-together now.

"Of course, it's Thursday," said Becky, "I'd forgotten. I'm feeling off it today. I'll have a word with Mr Azim."

Becky had looked pale all morning. I don't think she'd got back into the rhythm of school or perhaps it was a virus. She wheeled me to the Art Room. Mr Azim had arranged the chairs in a circle and no one else had arrived yet.

"Is it okay if I leave Lauren with you today?" said Becky.

"What? Yes, I don't see why not." He seemed a bit confused. "If you're happy with that, Lauren?"

Yes.

Jennifer and Emily walked in.

"Jennifer," said Mr Azim, "you can do yes and no with Lauren, can't you?"

"Yeah, sure," said Jennifer, brushing her hair out of her eyes.

"Off you go, Becky," said Mr Azim, "we'll manage without you today. I hope you get well soon."

"Thanks," Becky disappeared.

Mary joined the group. There was an arrangement of red roses and yellow freesias on a table in the centre of the room. I sneezed.

"Sorry about the flower smells," said Mr Azim, "it's a still life for the mock GCSE's and it has to stay exactly as it is. I thought we could start with what we did at Christmas. Lauren, you start. Did you have your family to stay?"

Yes.

"Did you enjoy it?"

No.

"I'm sorry about that but we can't go into it without Becky being here."

My cousin Grace listened to her iPod and played computer games all the time.

I'd remembered the Christmas when we'd played without words among the wrapping paper but that was years ago. It was nothing like that this time. The best thing was hearing the others sing carols while Grace played the tinkly piano in the lounge.

There was a knock on the door and Anthony walked in. I was amazed. I thought he must have made a mistake.

"Anthony, you've come to join us," said Mr Azim, "that's good but please try and be punctual; we don't have long."

Jennifer made a space and Anthony came and sat down next to me. I had decidedly mixed feelings. At the beginning I'd hoped that Anthony would want to be in the group but he'd be a big distraction.

"Am I right in thinking," said Mr Azim, "that you can help Lauren to speak, Anthony?"

"You mean FC?" said Anthony, like a pro, "yeah, I've done loads with Lauren."

Slight exaggeration.

"Lauren, would you be happy for Anthony to do FC for you today?"

Anthony picked up my hand so I could answer. I could feel him willing my finger to say yes.

No.

I wasn't ready for it; it felt like a minefield.

I needed to sort out my mixed-up feelings. Anthony looked crestfallen.

"Never mind. We're telling each other about what went on at Christmas, Anthony."

"I'm Mary, by the way. We had a quiet Christmas, because my brother was ill with a virus."

"What was the best thing?" said Mr Azim.

"Probably watching the Snowman film for the tenth time because we all sat together and afterwards we had mince pies and sparklers."

Jennifer and Emily talked about their family Christmas. Then it was Anthony's turn.

"We had champagne on Christmas day. Matt and I made a robot out of snow then we went sledging."

It was strange that Anthony hadn't mentioned his family but the snow seemed to loom much larger in his mind.

"I drove my family to London," said Mr Azim, "and the best thing was watching the children playing with their new toys. Right, Lauren, I had an idea over the holidays. What about playing twenty questions? Everyone happy with that?"

There were nods around the circle.

"You can start, Mary," said Mr Azim.

Mary and Anthony changed places. Mary picked up my hand and I just about signalled yes.

"We'll have five turns each doing yes and no with Lauren and we'll take it in turns to ask the questions, ready?"

There was a tension in the air at first with Anthony being there. Then people got more excited and tried to guess what I was thinking of. Anthony's hand felt different from everyone else's. I could sense the difference with my eyes closed. Anthony was faster than ever at picking up 'yes and no' which helped the guessing game move along.

We fitted in three rounds. Mr Azim summed up at the end of the session.

"Well done, everyone. Anthony, I'm pleased that you've started coming it's changed the whole atmosphere. Have you got any comments?"

"I was thinking how hard it would be to do a portrait of Lauren with her arms moving about all the time."

"True. Do you paint at all, Lauren?"

No.

Not since I was very young. Even then they weren't much more than scribbles. Anthony picked up my hand and the board.

****ing ****.*

He acted as if he owned me.

"What did she say?" said Jennifer.

"She swore," said Anthony.

I'm here. Don't talk like that about me.

"Why's that?"

"I dunno," said Anthony, "she swears all the time."

I bet you'd swear if people talked about you like that.

"Anyway we have to close now," said Mr Azim, "see you next week."

Julian came in; on time for once.

"Right," he said, "let's get you some lunch."

He wheeled me into the canteen and fortunately Anthony was still around when he got out the board.

"What is it?" he said.

I want to talk to Anthony.

"Anthony," said Julian, "can you join us over here?"

Anthony brought his tray over. He was half way through a plate with a sausage roll, chips and beans.

"Do you want me to do the FC?" said Julian.

Yes.

I could express myself a lot more clearly with Julian. FC took more effort with Anthony. I waited for him to sit down on the opposite side of the table. It was always noisy at lunchtime which made it harder for me to concentrate.

Why didn't you come to the café?

"Lauren, I apologised for that, that's it."

No. Answer please.

"I-had-an-emergency-dental-appointment." He spoke the words slowly and loudly as if I was an imbecile.

Honest answer please.

Anthony just shrugged his shoulders and swallowed his last few chips. He wasn't going to say.

Did you have second thoughts about spending time with someone in a wheelchair?

Anthony went a deep shade of beetroot. He looked at me out of the corner of his eyes. I took that as a 'yes'. I was right but he didn't want to say it out loud. He didn't deny it.

"I'll just go and get a dessert," he said and went off to the serving hatch.

My feelings for Anthony had grown without me wanting them to. Did I have to let him be my friend just because he was the only person who'd taken the trouble to learn FC?

He wasn't like the boy I'd had in mind at all; he was too immature and indecisive and too full of contradictions. I knew he liked me but I guessed that he was put off by the wheelchair, the carers and everything I needed. I wanted someone to tell me: 'If you've only got one person to choose and he's a long way from ideal should you stick with that person or give up?'

That night, Marian came to visit. She stretched out on the cream armchair in the lounge. Mum had lit a fire and the logs turned into red hot embers. Marian picked up my hand and the board.

"How's things?"

The work's fine. Maths is better now that Mr Todd accepts I do the homework.

"Good, yes, Sarah told me about that."

I go shopping with Jennifer and Emily and Jennifer is getting good at doing yes and no.

"What about FC?"

There's one boy, Anthony, who's –

Mum came in with a tray of mugs of tea and plates of flapjack.

"Anthony," said Mum. "you've spoken to him again?"

Only briefly. He didn't say much.

"Is that the boy who didn't come to the café?" said Marian. "How do you feel about him?"

I'm not sure.

I didn't want to say in front of Mum. I felt angry but I was delighted that he'd come to join the group. I thought I might get to know him better. Mum and Marian had their drinks and talked over old times. When Mum went out I had a chance to talk to Marian again.

I might be in love.

"Well mixed feelings are fine in romance," said Marian. "But you have to keep your head screwed on right and look out for people's faults."

That made me laugh: Anthony had plenty of faults. I could feel his fear long before he held my hand. He could be arrogant, clumsy and self-centred but he had moments of truly listening and speaking from the heart.

I'll do that.

"I'm sure you will; I know how important the academic side is to you."

Anthony came to the following get-togethers and I dreamed about him, a sure sign that he'd entered my subconscious. I could call up an image of him in my mind and watch him doing his favourite things: I imagined him lying back on a bean bag on the floor of his bedroom playing computer games, drawing, painting, running up stairs and having a shower.

I'd never been to his house but he described it as an ex-council house shaped like a child's drawing of a house with a chimney at each end. He played badminton over the washing line in the back garden which sloped steeply uphill. He played shooting games with water pistols in summer and BB guns and laser guns in winter. He loved to go karting and his ambition was to drive a car as soon as he was able to.

Of all the things he mentioned, there weren't any that I could join in with, except perhaps bird watching. He and Matt had done a Little Owl survey and they went around town at night playing a recording of an owl shrieking to tell if there were any males around. He said they heard a male calling in the willow trees just above my house.

Mr Azim stopped me and Julian in the corridor four weeks into term

"Lauren, I was thinking about you painting," he said. "Why don't you come to the Sketch Club tonight, just to see what it's like."

Okay.

I'd been hoping I'd bump into him. I knew that Anthony went to Sketch Club so I agreed straight away.

Thank you, Mr Azim.

"What for? I'm just doing my job."

I wanted to thank you for running the get-togethers. I couldn't have managed without them.

"I'm glad they've made a difference."

Definitely. Lots of good things have come out of the group.

"I'm touched," said Mr Azim.

Did you know Marian Henderson?

His eyes went wide.

"Marian, yes, of course, that was ages ago. Is she a friend of yours?"

She taught me how to speak.

"I had no idea. She's a very talented person."

I could put you two in touch.

"That's a lovely idea, Lauren, I'll have a think about whether I'd like to take up that offer. See you later today."

Julian took me through to the quad and stopped at the pond.

"What are you up to, Lauren?" he said. "Are you running a dating agency now?"

I just wanted to thank him, that's all.

I wouldn't have tried that with Becky; it was Julian's laid-back approach that encouraged me.

Later on that day, he guided me up the ramp to the Art Room. There was a still life of fruit in the centre of the room. Matt had set up his easel and Anthony was hesitating over where to put his stool. Julian found a chair and set up the board.

"What's your favourite colour, Lauren?" said Mr Azim.

Magenta, claret, crimson, port wine and maroon.

Mr Azim smiled and showed a full set of teeth. "I see, like the colour of your chair?"

The room was filling with the smell of turpentine as five different people squeezed out tubes of colours onto their palettes.

Of course. I chose it

"Would you like to have a go at painting?" said Mr Azim.

Yes, I'd love to.

"If you come here next week –"

"Sir, that's half term," said Liz.

"True, I mean in two weeks' time, we can set it all up for you."

Fine.

I sat on the terrace and watched the shadows shift between the apple and pear trees in the lower garden. Mr Azim was my hero. He was a real artist, sensual and open at the same time. I couldn't wait until the following Thursday when I'd get to paint with Anthony.

I liked talking to Anthony, even if I said the wrong thing. He let me say things I'd never said before. I never dreamed of feeling like this about a boy.

All through the Thursday lessons I kept thinking about Sketch Club.

I had no idea what Mr Azim had in mind but I trusted him to find a way that I could join in which was all I wanted, being in the Art Room during lunch hour made it worse. I noticed two fantasy pictures of Anthony's: a sword fighting dragon and a golden dawn over a ruined castle.

The Art Room was empty at three thirty so Julian and I waited for everyone else to arrive.

"Anthony's good at painting, isn't he?" said Julian.

The clock ticked slowly. A fruit bowl stood on a lime green tablecloth. The apple looked dried up and the banana had gone blotchy.

There were voices outside in the corridor. Then Matt and Anthony and the others arrived, with Mr Azim close behind.

They all picked out their half-finished pictures and started setting up.

"Who would you like to mix the colours for you, Lauren?"

Anthony.

"Oh, alright then," he said; he didn't sound keen.

"Excellent," said Mr Azim. "Here's your chance, Anthony. I want to see some pure tones and using just three colours if you can."

He took off his blazer and tie, loosened the top button of his shirt and put an apron on. Then he picked up my hand.

I need an apron too, Anthony.

He struggled to release the sleeve of my blazer.

"Pull," said Julian.

Anthony pulled the sleeve hard. He probably thought I was deliberately making it difficult.

"Harder," said Julian, laughing.

My blazer came loose and Anthony nearly fell over. His hands brushed my face as he put the loop of the apron over my head.

Julian lifted me forward and Anthony's face came close to mine again while he tied the apron at the back. I felt his breath on my cheek and his aftershave filled my lungs.

"There," said Julian, lifting my hair out of her eyes. He manoeuvred the chair so that I could reach the easel.

"Right, let's start," said Mr Azim. "Remember: colour, tone, depth. Only use a few colours, four at the most."

A concentrated silence fell as five people started measuring the distances with a brush at arm's length. Matt let out little grunts as he sized his picture up.

Start with mossy green.

Anthony sat on a wooden stool on my left. He chose tubes of paint: red, blue, yellow and white. Prompted by me, he mixed the colours for the background and the fruit: greens, light and dark, lemony greens for the apple, pinkish red for the streaks. He alternated between mixing the colours and doing FC.

"Five minute break," said Mr Azim.

"Is it that the time already?" said Anthony.

"You spend hours mixing the colours, don't you?" said Julian.

"Yeah."

Anthony stretched his back and then got back into colour mixing with light and dark shades of yellow and making a whitest white for the highlights. He found a deep sea green for the shadows.

"It's quite fun, this," he said.

He slid the palette knife back and forth to make circles of matching and clashing colours.

118

He held a blob of paint on the end of the knife in front of me so that I could compare it with the real thing.

More red.

He mixed in some red and showed me the result.

Perfect.

"You should be getting the colours in by now," said Mr Azim.

Anthony handed the brush to Julian and he exaggerated my gestures so that the brush made strokes on the hardboard that served as a canvas. I called out noisily. My arms moved about unpredictably. Blobs of paint landed on my apron. The still life emerged as a series of thick diagonal lines made by slashing movements in roughly the right place.

Darkest dark.

I put the shadow under the orange.

Brightest bright.

Anthony had a different look in his eye, like a fox. He kept blinking and widening his eyes and he kept still. I envied the fruit, it had his full attention. Mr Azim stepped around the circle. "Fill the canvas," he said, but mostly he watched in silence. People swallowed, people held their breath.

Anthony can do the final touch.

He leaned over and held my hand so the white paint made a highlight on the orange and the apples. I took aim with my tight muscles to bring the brush close to the painting.

"More?"

Yes.

"Finished?"

Yes.

Anthony put our painting against the wall with everyone else's then he washed up.

"I like yours, Lauren," Liz said.

"Lauren," said Anthony, "you've got some paint on your neck."

He dipped a cloth in the solvent and waited for me to turn my head away then he dabbed my skin.

"That's better."

It was hot in the Art Room after all that concentration. I had never realised painting was so sensual. Mr Azim walked along the row of pictures, commenting on each one.

"That's good, Matt." he said. "That restricted palette works very well."

"Good brushwork, Liz. That's a lot freer than your other paintings."

"Jake, you've really captured the colouring of the apple."

Then he came to our painting.

"This is quite extraordinary," he said. "It's complete and yet it's all suggested."

"It's like looking through frosted glass," said Liz.

"It is," said Mr Azim. "Are you happy with it?"

No.

"Really, why not?"

I didn't cover the canvas.

Mr Azim shrugged his shoulders. "It was your first oil painting. Well done, Lauren. And Anthony, your colour mixing has really come on."

I had to keep looking at the painting. Did I really paint that?

"Thanks, Lauren," said Anthony, "that was more fun than I was expecting."

"We're late," said Mr Azim. "See you all next week." He switched off the light before we'd gone out of the door.

Mum's driving on the way home was erratic. It wasn't my fault that Julian hadn't told her I was staying on.

I waited in the kitchen while Mum put the shopping away. She found some oil paint on my blouse.

"You're not going there again," she said.

That wasn't so bad. It was fun painting but I didn't think I'd have the energy to paint every week. Anyway, Anthony needed time on his own. I relived the magical feeling of painting with Anthony while Mum picked up the post. I was ready to open up to Anthony and it frightened me. I could get hurt.

Mum read the second half of Midsummer Night's Dream and it was a welcome distraction. It was the wrong season to hear about bees drinking nectar but it felt warm and romantic. I could just do with a mossy hill to lay down on so I could fall asleep. And whose voice would I hear when I opened my eyes? A squeaky half broken voice. A boy with a hairless chest: Anthony.

Chapter 10

Practically all my class came to the evening Assembly about the Duke of Edinburgh Award. Paintings from the A level projects lined the walls. I sat with Mum at the front of the hall. Anthony was at the back with his mates.

"Are there any parents here with First Aid skills?" said Mr Preston.

A man stood up behind us.

"I've got a resuscitation training certificate," he said. He sounded like a science professor; could he be Anthony's Dad?

"That's very handy," said Mr Preston. "Any parents willing to act as stewards, see me afterwards or contact me via email."

The man behind us scratched away with his pen taking down the email address.

"There are four elements to the D of E," said Mr Preston. The room went dark, he clicked up a slide presentation and pictures came up of activities from previous years: abseiling, paragliding, skiing and trampolining.

Mr Preston talked about volunteering, there were pictures of visiting an old people's home and helping at a Stroke Club. Next up was a picture I recognised.

"Here are our volunteers helping out at an after school gymnastics session."

It was the gym at the Special School I went to for half a term. It took me straight back to the sounds and smells, the efficient, caring teachers and the swampy feeling of low expectations.

No one took GCSE's there. The head teacher was dead proud of the music room where a few random key presses made a tune. The most you could hope for was a credit for getting dressed in the ADL suite, a mock-up bedroom and kitchen they had for sixth formers.

"And a skill," said Mr Preston. "Ice skating, playing the clarinet, cross country running."

All the activities he showed were for active people with no disabilities.

"And finally, the expedition," said Mr Preston. "We've never had to cancel, though we have had some pretty extreme conditions." Pictures appeared of curtains of rain and bedraggled walkers weighed down with equipment. "It's best if you make up groups of six to do the expedition together. Make sure they're people you can spend forty eight hours with, though. When you reach the camp site, you'll divide into girls' and boys' tents."

When the talk was over, Mum wheeled me to the front. We had to wait until Mr Preston had spoken to the man who'd been behind us. He looked like a typical professor with lop-sided glasses and uncombed hair.

"I can bring some rehydration fluids," he said.

I coughed and he turned and frowned at me. I suppose he thought I should have covered my mouth but I can't do that.

"Fine, thank you, Mr Roberts," said Mr Preston. "That would be a great help."

Mum advanced my chair and got the board out.

What can I do in place of the expedition?

"Hi Lauren, it's good to see you here," said Mr Preston. "Here's what I've found on wheelchair expeditions."

He clicked some buttons and brought up a D of E page listing the ways teams of people with a wheelchair user could visit historic sites, film their activities, keep a diary and report back on access.

Fine if I can persuade people to go with me.

"I'll make sure the numbers are even between all the groups. Give me your email address and I'll send you this page."

Mum wheeled me across to the back of the hall where Anthony was standing with Emily and Jennifer. Then she wandered off to talk to the other mums that she knew.

"Righto, Anthony," said Mr Roberts. His jaw dropped as he looked at the girls. "Helloo, I'm Anthony's Dad and you're…"

"I'm Emily, this is Jennifer and Lauren."

Mr Roberts completely ignored me, staring in stead at Emily's hiked up skirt.

"Good to meet you," he said. Anthony was covering his face with embarrassment.

"It's a tough ask, as they say, the Bronze Award," his dad went on, "there's a lot of heavy equipment to carry. Are you sure you two would be able to carry it off? You're so slender."

"Oh, I think so," said Emily, adjusting her glasses and miming hill walking with her legs. "I've been walking in Scotland."

"Really?" said Mr Roberts, looking hypnotised by Emily's actions. "Which part?"

"All over," said Emily, "the Shetlands, Hebrides, Arran."

"The islands?"

"Yeah, Ben Nevis especially,"

"I would never have believed it," he said. "Nice to talk to you, Emily and - Jennifer. I've volunteered to be a steward so I may see you on the day. Anyway, Anthony, it's time to be movin' on."

When his Dad was out of earshot, he said:

"Sorry about that. He's bonkers, my Dad."

"Oh, I thought it was hilarious," said Emily.

"Did you make up all those places?" said Anthony.

Emily covered her mouth and rocked her shoulders in cartoon fashion. Anthony followed his dad. Jennifer laughed loudly.

"We could be a team," said Jennifer, "starting with you, me, Lauren, Liz and Jake. Do you think Anthony would join us?"

Yes. No

"You mean you'd like him to join us," said Jennifer, "but on thinking about it he probably wouldn't?"

Yes.

We both laughed. Jennifer had reconstructed my thoughts from two movements of my fingers.

"Can I come round to your house?" said Jennifer.

Yes.

"I want to try out all these fancy gadgets you've got."

Mum rejoined us.

"Why don't you come next week, Jennifer?" said Mum.

Anthony's Mum came to speak to me and Mum.

"Is this your daughter?" she said.

"Yes, this is Lauren," said Mum.

"Hello, Lauren," she said. "Oh, you look just like a doll, don't you?"

She picked up my hand without asking. Get off me, you stink. She was wearing a particularly obnoxious perfume.

"Do you have any other children?"

"No," said Mum, "one is quite enough."

"Yes, I'm sure you've got your hands full with Lauren," she said. "I'm Helen Roberts, by the way, Anthony Roberts' Mum."

Poor Anthony.

"Does Anthony have any brothers or sisters?" said Mum.

"Yes, actually, Vicky's sixteen and she's taking nine GCSEs. She's quite academic. Not like Anthony."

I sang the Blue Danube to myself, anything to block out this nonsense.

The next day Becky brought me over to speak to Anthony when we were waiting to go into class. He did the FC.

Are you doing the award?

"Yeah, we're all doing it: me, Matt, Liz, Jake and Dan. We just need one more person for the expedition."

That's good.

"Yeah, Matt is going to be our map reader. Did you come along to hear about it, then?

No, I'm doing it too.

"No way. I don't - how?"

Anthony's ignorance was deeply offensive.

I spoke to Mr Preston. He said I could.

"What? Including the voluntary work?"

I'm going to chat to the ladies at the Rest Home. You could help me.

"No thanks, Lauren. For the activity, I'm doing gymnastics with Jake."

I felt the anger rising inside me. Anthony was completely unaware of how he was insulting me with his ignorance.

"What about you?"

I'm doing Eurythmy.

"The Eurythmics, that's a band, isn't it?"

No. Music and movement. Rudolph Steiner invented it.

"Oh, okay. I'm doing an animation course with Matt for the skill part. But Dad says I have to raise the money myself. I'm starting on Sunday, selling some DVD's at the Racecourse car boot."

I'm doing sailing.

He shook his head as if he couldn't believe how I could possibly do that. I focus on the things I can do, not the rest.

"I'd love to go sailing," he said.

Perhaps you will.

"But what about the expedition?

Don't be so obnoxious. Go away.

I'm up to here with your patronising attitude, Anthony. You need educating.

I can't do it all by myself. Why don't you do Disability Politics as a skill? People like to stand on their own two feet even when they can't stand.

I don't see why you can't join me at the Rest Home. It would be an education for you to meet the old dears. They'd love it if you could bear to smile at them. You're just like your Dad: rude, offensive and thick. I was steaming with anger through the whole of the school day. It's infuriating; I could only speak when people let me. The rest of the time I had to simmer like a volcano that couldn't explode.

I went home and thought about Anthony's words.

Mum hoisted me into the bath. There's a poster in the bathroom with a group of disabled campaigners in front of a double decker bus, it says: 'We're here: Deal with it.'

It still inspires me when I'm enjoying the floaty feeling of the water up to my shoulders. Mum sits in the chair and reads a book while I muse. Fact number one: Anthony likes me. Fact number two: Anthony insults me every time we talk. I needed to have a show-down. Was he capable of learning?

Mum hoisted me out, dried me, dressed me and popped me back in the comfortable chair in my study.

"What would you like for tea?" she said.

Can I go to the Racecourse on Sunday?

"Becky will be here; I'm going to church. Why do you want to go there, anyway?"

Anthony's selling some stuff. I need to talk to him.

"Alright then, I'll let Becky know if that's what you really want."

It is.

Chapter 11

"I've got the hospital trust to agree I can view your medical records," said Mum.

We were sitting in the lounge listening to Radio 3.

"The delay was all about whether they could accept your consent if you gave it by FC. Ryan's Mum says I'm taking it all too seriously. Anyway, we'll be bale to find out who, of all the specialists you've seen will speak up for FC. We're visiting the hospital next week to read your notes. We can't take them off the premises but there's a room where I can read through them. You'll have to come with me."

I can't say I was pleased. Everything to do with hospitals: disinfectant smells that got up your nose, walls painted in pastel shades of yellow and green, echoing footsteps in the corridor, the bracing wind in the gaps between the buildings, all reminded me of the months I'd spent waiting for a hip operation and suffering from a chest infection.

To be honest I'd have preferred not to sit exams with specially qualified invigilators. Some people's university courses depended just on judgements of their teachers; that was fine by me. But it was a big issue for Mum so I went along with it.

Mum parked on the yellow crisscross at the hospital entrance.

We went to the reception desk.

"Medical Records? It's in the Castleton building, in the blue zone, first floor," said the lady.

Once we got beyond the shopping arcade foyer, it was the same tangle of anonymous corridors I remembered from years back. Judging by the number of people who we passed staring at maps or looking vacant, the directions and signposting hadn't improved.

Mum was used to the building so we slid along the corridors, out through double doors, between stilts that supported snaking first floor corridors, into the red zone. We passed the sign for the Neonatal Intensive Care Unit. I imagined myself being wheeled along at night in a lit-up incubator like some alien form of life. Would I have noticed the cream-coloured walls? Six months I'd spent fighting for my life there. There might be similar 'blue babies' like me struggling to survive at that moment behind those closed doors. Fifteen years later and I'm still on wheels.

We crossed into the orange zone, familiar territory of operating theatres and recovery rooms from later years: procedures to release tendons and free up damaged joints. The longer I spent in those buildings the heavier I felt. We carried on following the little blue square like travellers of old.

Mum made a couple of unexpected right angle turns to find the lift which let us out on the first floor. We arrived at the Medical Records Department and I gave my consent. The lady from Medical Records looked bewildered; I don't suppose they'd had anyone like me coming to read their notes.

Mum settled down with two massive files in the windowless Interview Room.

The walls were the uniform shade of beige and the circular white clock which was balanced on the only table read half past midnight. Mum sat at the table turning the pages of an overflowing file which said:

Lauren Stark   N504938726   Volume I

'Confidential: Must not be Handled by the Patient.'

The air conditioning was humming continually but the temperature was rising. After half an hour, Mum had filled a foolscap page with quotes from various experts who had seen me from birth up to eight years old.

"This is what I've got so far," she read.

'Lauren has advanced cerebral palsy as a result of brain damage during a prolonged labour. She has a spastic quadriplegia with choreo-athetosis that has increased in intensity during her first eight years of life.'

"So that's why you were able to drive your wheelchair when you were young but you can't do it now. I thought it was just that you'd become stronger but it says here that the involuntary movements got worse as you grew up."

I wasn't that amazed.

'Lauren's visual fields and acuity are difficult to determine due to nystagmus and a lack of cooperation. She demonstrates persistent neonatal reflexes such as a startle response which is easily elicited by sudden noises such as a hand-clap.'

I remember them clapping their hands and squeezing my finger nails.

"Really?" said Mum. "I don't."

'She has never acquired the normal protective reflexes in the tongue and throat. Consequently, Lauren's life expectancy is short on account of a severe risk of aspiration which is the likely cause of death.'

"What does that mean?"   Mum turned to me. "What's the matter, Lauren?"

My lower lip was trembling.

I sound like a machine that's not working.

"That's right, they're talking about stupid reflexes that don't matter. Who cares if you've got a grasp reflex? It's quite handy. I can give you things to hold onto. They're not interested in what you are able to do. It's disgusting."

Mum was raising her voice. She pulled the case notes towards her.

"Listen to this: 'Aged 8, Lauren has a mental age of six months and can be expected to remain retarded for the rest of her life.' That's what Dr Collins, the paediatrician said, and he was so nice to us at the time."

I love your anger.

"Hmm, maybe, but it's doing my head in. Look at this letter to the headmaster of your primary school:

"'Lauren's mother is overprotective and deluded about Lauren's intellectual capacity. I fear that she will be severely disappointed when Lauren's advanced cognitive impairment becomes obvious.'

"What a bastard. And he sent copies to Marian, the GP, the clinical psychologist and the occupational therapist. I cannot believe it."

Mum flicked through more pages of letters while I listened to the second hand on the clock ticking.

After twenty minutes I attracted Mum's attention.

Does it explain how I can have sex?

"I'm afraid it doesn't say much about that here, Lauren."

Mum flicked through the clinic letters at the back.

"Here's what it says under "Genito-urinary System", for what it's worth:

132

"'In contrast to other reflexes, the labial reflex is intact. This implies that should Lauren survive into puberty she is likely to manifest a normal sexual drive. However, her sexual disinhibition will almost certainly give rise to serious ethical and behavioural problems. Da-da-da Consultant Neurologist.'

"He goes on to recommend removal of the ovaries. What do you think of that?"

Bollocks. It's like 1920's America.

Mum seemed to be going over the old ground again which didn't surprise me. She loved to take on the establishment.

What's the most recent letter?

She opened volume two and leafed through the letters.

"Oh my God. Listen to this."

"'Lauren is now fourteen years old. I remain extremely sceptical of Lauren's ability to communicate. It is impossible to know how much of Lauren's so-called communication is down to her and how much is attributable to her somewhat pushy mother. I have been unable to demonstrate any voluntary component to the movements of her upper limbs.

"Examination reveals postural reflex activity alone. I can only conclude that Lauren's use of the letter board is entirely factitious and any opinions which attributed to Lauren are to be treated with extreme caution."

"What are these people here for?" said Mum. "What do they achieve by this?"

I switched off. I learnt a long time ago to concentrate on the feelings of people that matter to me. I know I can't change the opinions of professionals by arguing with them.

Imagine bringing all the doctors and psychologists into a room to educate them. *'You talk about me as if I'm a child but I'm not. I can decide who I want to spend time with and who I want to have sex with. You're supposed to be helping me.'*

There'd be a riot; they wouldn't believe me.

"Let's have a cup of coffee and think about this," said Mum.

Uniformed staff passed us with jangling keys. Every door had a combination lock or a card reader. It was more like a prison than a hospital.

In the canteen, Mum turned and followed my gaze.

"Look at her," she nodded towards a young woman speed-walking past with a name badge clipped to her breast pocket, "arrogant bitch. I'd like to tie that stethoscope round her neck."

I was actually looking at a woman in a red coat that I remembered seeing before. It was Mrs Roberts, of course, queuing at the counter.

What could she possibly be doing in hospital? Had Anthony had an accident?

All my anger about Anthony's ignorance drained away and I suddenly felt anxious about him.

"Ma," I tried to attract Mum's attention but she dismissed the sounds I was making as just the usual noises.

Mrs Roberts paid for a drink and went away without Mum noticing. Maybe she worked in the hospital; she's some kind of social worker.

You've taken me seriously for once, Anthony, and beamed yourself onto another planet. I was suddenly filled with a panic I'd never known before. Are you never going to speak to me again?

134

Mum put my coat on. When all the specialists say I'm stupid I need people around me who believe me, especially when Mum's turning a crisis into a disaster.

Had I been mean to Anthony? He's got to learn to treat me like a human being.

"Let's go," said Mum.

Mission failed.

Next day, Anthony wasn't in Maths when the lesson started. I was started feeling anxious about what had happened when he came in late.

He looked okay; he wasn't limping and I couldn't see any scratches or bruises. I wasn't able to have a word with him until the mid-morning break when we cornered him in the canteen.

Are you okay?

"Yeah, fine, why do you ask?"

I saw your Mum at the hospital last night.

"Yeah, I was there too. My Dad fell off his bike."

Seriously?

"Yeah. He broke his funny bone. He's back home now. What about you, what were you doing there?"

Calling up my medical notes to find FC supporters.

"Sounds like football fans. And?"

None of the doctors believe in FC.

He shrugged his shoulders. He didn't have much idea what I was talking about.

"Or vampires and zombies."

How pathetic. You've no idea.

Don't laugh.

Jennifer came round to my house after school on Wednesday.

We did our homework on the American War of Independence together. She was amazed at how long it took to write a hundred words using FC.

She loved going up in the lift and letting Becky swing her about in the hoist.

"It's a shame you can't control it with your brain waves, Lauren," she said.

"We've got a toy that works on brainwaves," said Becky.

"Cool."

"Do you want to have a go?"

"Sure."

Becky set up the headphones which communicated to a circular pad in the middle of the floor. A table tennis ball floated up in the air and stayed suspended in the upward flow from a fan. I made it go down and then up again.

"Oh wow," said Jennifer. "That's you doing that? Let me try."

Jennifer got the hang of it after a while.

"But I can't do it as quickly as you can, Lauren."

I've had plenty of practice.

After tea, Jennifer and I spent some time in the garden while Mum loaded the dishwasher. I felt as if I was floating on air, sitting wordlessly with my friend taking in everything I could hear.

"It's been fantastic, Lauren, can I come again soon?"

Yes.

I indicated yes twice to mean 'yes, please.'

"About Anthony – "

I was suddenly worried about what she was about to say.

"You know we play around a lot and I've known him a long time," she said.

My shoulders tensed up. I didn't want to know; had he promised to go out with her?

Yes?

"I won't get in the way of your friendship with him. I can see it's very precious to you."

I relaxed again; Jennifer was a real friend. We sat there for a while watching the birds flying in and out of the nest box in the apple tree.

It was after eight o'clock on Sunday morning when Becky and I approached the racecourse in the van. A mass migration of punters filled the pavements. People with buggies loaded with toys and black bags full of tools headed in one direction while the eager latecomers dodged around them and headed towards the racecourse with their wheelie suitcases and backpacks.

We joined the queue of cars and Becky reversed into a tight space a fair distance from the entrance. She guided my chair onto the tarmac paths that divided the first few rows of stalls. We found Anthony in the less favoured zone, four rows back where the path was full of tyre tracks and muddy pools.

Mr Roberts sat on the car bumper behind a wallpapering table supported by boxes in the middle. Anthony and Vicky stood on either side trying to interest passers by in DVD's, soft toys and cosmetics.

"Lauren," said Vicky. "Would you like to try some quick dry nail varnish? They're really good if you can't keep still."

No.

"She says no thanks," said Becky.

Mr Roberts stood up too quickly and banged his head on the roof of the boot.

"Ow, Lauren," he said, rubbing the top of his head, "I've heard all about you." The wind was blowing his wayward hair about.

"And I'm Becky, Lauren's LSA."

"Hello, Becky. Can I see how Lauren communicates with you, Anthony?"

Anthony came round beside me. My heart sank as Becky passed him the board and he crouched beside my chair.

"You see," he said, "it's a printed-out keyboard with 'yes' in one corner and 'no' in the other," he picked up my hand, "and if I hold Lauren's hand like this – "

He made it sound like a magic trick.

Half a minute in and he was already annoying me intensely. Crouching is a bad position to try and do FC in.

For a while nothing happened then my finger started darting all over the board. Anthony read out the words.

I can say whatever I like.

"Wait a minute," said Mr Roberts, "that's you doing it."

Yes.

"What?" said Anthony. His face went red. He obviously thought the answer was no. Serve him right.

It was Anthony.

"It was Anthony," he'd spoken my words before he realised what I meant. He turned to me. "How can you say that?"

I was furious. When speaking takes so much effort you at least hope that people are going to pay attention to what you say.

"I knew it," said Mr Roberts. "I read it in the paper, FC has been debunked. It's a hoax."

I was in an impossible situation. Anthony was angry with me and his Dad was laughing at me.

"Oh, well," said Mr Roberts, "it's more interesting than I thought."

"It's real," said Anthony but even he didn't sound convinced. I watched him clamping his jaw tightly shut. Becky took over the FC while Mr Roberts was packing a pile of unsold books into a cardboard box.

Vicky, can I have a look at the nail varnish?

"Sure," she passed over three mini bottles. "There's dusky mauve, strawberry ice cream and neon pink."

Becky held them up in front of my eyes while my head went from side to side. They looked glittery and thick.

"They're scented as well," said Vicky. "They haven't been opened and they dry in forty seconds."

Mr Roberts was stacking boxes into the boot of the car.

How much are they?

"Fifty pence now."

I'd like dusky mauve, please.

Becky found my purse and put the nail varnish into my backpack.

Anthony, would you like to come for a walk round the lake?

Mr Roberts looked up. It was silly but he made me feel like a fraud.

"We're all having a meal at the carvery," he said. "Becky, you and Lauren could come and join us if you like."

No.

I needed to talk to Anthony and I wasn't going to be patronised by this horrible man.

"We're fine, thanks, Mr Roberts," said Becky.

"Anthony," said Mr Roberts, "won't you join us for lunch? It'll be roast beef with Yorkshire pudding and a dessert."

I turned to Anthony; he was reading the back of a CD. If you go with your Dad, I thought, I'll never speak to you again. He put his head on one side as if he was seriously considering going.

"Not this time, thanks Dad," he said. He leaned over and whispered in my ear: "Sorry, my Dad can be a total wanker."

I laughed. Anthony preferred a walk with me to a nice lunch. But did he realise what was coming?

Cars were revving up around us and starting to drive off in clouds of smoke. Mr Roberts got into the front of his car and Vicky climbed in on the passenger side. His Dad reversed out and wound the window down.

"Are you sure, Anthony?" he said.

"Definitely, I'll make my own way back."

The car lurched over the ruts and Vicky waved at me as she went by.

"The FC goes to pot when Lauren's upset," said Becky. "It still happens to me and I've been doing it for years."

Becky guided my chair onto the limestone chippings and along the pavement. When we reached the car park at the country park, Becky got out the board and took my glove off to do FC.

"Shall I give you two some time on your own?" she said.

Yes. Come back in an hour.

Then she put my glove back on.

"I'll go for a walk round the lake," said Becky. "I'll see you back here at one o'clock, alright? Call me if you want to come back sooner, bye."

Anthony drove my chair out of the car park and followed the path towards the lake. He must have switched the gears up to maximum because he raced up the muddy path. I didn't mind, the chair's never tipped over though it did slide in the melted frost.

He paused for a moment to recover his breath at the top of the dyke.

"I didn't think it would get up here. It's such a steep slope."

He shielded his eyes from the sun with his arm.

"Look at that."

The sun reflected off the lake behind the islands of trees. A boat rocked gently in the silver water. A row of gulls stood on a weir that ran across one corner of the lake. Anthony got the board out and took my right hand glove off.

You upset me.

I sounded miserable but I couldn't stop.

"When?"

At the D of E.

"You mean about the expedition?"

Exactly. I go camping. I've been to Glastonbury.

"Glastonbury? Who was playing?"

The Darkness, the White Stripes, the Arctic Monkeys.

"You saw all those?"

Did you think it would be past my bedtime?

"I'm sorry."

It was the second time I'd heard him apologise. I felt a wave of warmth flow through me which threatened to melt the anger I'd been feeling.

Kiss me.

"Lauren, there's people around."

I couldn't see anyone.

Let's go opposite the island.

Spoilsport.   Anthony picked up my glove up and put it back on.

The chair's wheels skidded and tore at the meadow grass as it lurched along the dyke. We followed the path down the slope to a mini beach.   Anthony parked the chair by a bench under some trees and sat down. The finely cut grass was covered in goose pooh. You can't have everything.

"Is this alright?"

Who are you hiding from?

"Nobody, why?"

Camo trousers.

"Oh, right," said Anthony, "I just like the colour. You're wearing the necklace."

Yes. I love it.

A flock of geese came by overhead.

"You were right; I did worry about being seen with you in a wheelchair. But now I just think – "

Anthony put the board away and put his arm around my shoulder.

"It's cold," he said, "can I put my hand inside your coat?"

He lifted my finger and I hesitated to answer.

Yes.

His other hand was pulling me towards him. He wanted me close. It was a beautiful moment; his hands were cold but they warmed up quickly.

He lifted my hand and put it around his neck inside his parka. It was exactly what I needed; his neck was lovely and warm. Then he rested his hand on my shoulder inside my blouse.

A magpie flew past us towards an island of trees that was about twenty yards away.

I relaxed into the scene, the ice blue sky and the monochrome landscape. Anthony twisted my body towards him so that I was facing him. Shivers ran down my spine. I thought: 'Let's stay like this forever'. Very slowly, his lips were approaching mine and I tried to lift my head.

But it wasn't the right moment. My body objected. My legs kicked out together and went into painful spasms. I nearly kicked a black Labrador was sniffing around my wheelchair.

"Eeek," I screamed.

Anthony extracted his arm from my clothes and stood up.

"What's the matter?" he said. He sounded really spooked. "Lauren, are you okay?"

Bizarrely, I started giggling despite the cramping pain in my thighs. I didn't know if it was the absurdity of the situation or my emotions which were capable of switching all the time between pain and joy, happy and sad.

"What's the matter?"

Voices were coming closer. Anthony got the board out but I couldn't point to any letters. There was no way I could tell him what had happened. I was in too much pain. I screamed again and giggled some more.

Anthony grabbed hold of my shoulders and tried to lift me up. He obviously wasn't used to handling people like me.

He grabbed hold of the belt of my jeans and after a few tries and more screams he was able to shift me into a more comfortable position and my legs settled down.

A family with a young child and a dog came along the path and stopped beside the bench. I tried to work out whether it was an accident. Had my body objected to Anthony being close because I hadn't forgiven him for standing me up? The father tore up strips of bread.

"Here, give these to the ducks," he said.

"Daddy, what was that boy doing?"

"Don't worry," said his father, "here's comes a big white swan."

Anthony reached down beside me to put the board away. I could feel his level of tension rising as the boy's father watched him closely. Anthony switched on the chair and drove me further along the lake. He spoke once we were out of earshot.

"Phew, I'm glad that man didn't say anything."

I laughed heartily. Poor Anthony: caught between desire and self conscious embarrassment. The sun came out and a bumblebee hummed past. Anthony turned the chair around and headed back. It could have been my best day for years except for the painful spasms.

"We're late," he said as we approached the car park.

"Hi," said Becky. "I saw you by the lake."

Anthony seemed to shrink.

"Did you see those people swimming across?"

"Were they naturists?" said Anthony.

"No, they had trunks and bikinis on. They were right beside where you stopped."

"No," said Anthony. "We must have been looking the other way."

Anthony touched the back of my wrist and Becky took over controlling the chair. Is that it? I didn't want to kiss him but a hug would have been reassuring.

Chapter 12

Anthony came over before English to speak to me.

"What are you doing after school?"

The question rocked me back in the chair. What did he have in mind? Becky stepped aside and Anthony got the board out. Maybe he was thinking about canoodling under the conker trees.

Shopping, worst luck.

"Don't you like shopping?"

Not supermarket. It's boring. Mum takes me round but it's too crowded.

"Can I come?"

Why?

It was a daft idea.

"Let me ask your Mum. I could take you out in the chair."

I wasn't keen. There wasn't much to see in a supermarket car park: the recycling bins and trolley shelters.

"Don't you trust me to control the chair?"

Good point, he'd probably scrape the chair down one of the parked cars. It was touching that Anthony wanted to spend time with me but it wasn't like going out. Becky said her goodbyes as soon as Mum arrived.

"Errm, Mrs Stark," said Anthony, "I wondered if I could come shopping with you. I could take Lauren out in the chair."

"It won't be very interesting," she said. "How will you get home?"

"By bus."

"It's a bit cold."

"Ah," I waved my arm to show I wanted to speak.

"Don't pay any attention to the sounds she makes, they don't mean anything. Is that what you want, Lauren?"

Yes, Mum.

Stop putting me down.

"There's a path that leads through to the canal," said Anthony.

I'd seen the canal from the road but I'd never been down that way.

"Alright then, Anthony, but let your parents know where you are."

Anthony tapped away on his mobile while Mum used the tail lift and fixed my chair to the floor with straps. Anthony climbed in. He had to lean over me to clip the seat belt over my shoulder. I drank in his aftershave. He was so close I could feel his heart beating.

We held hands while Mum drove through town. Anthony didn't speak. It wasn't quite like the dream I'd had of friends occupying the seat beside me on the way to a day out.

Mum parked up and let Anthony work the controls on the tail lift. She obviously thought he'd be taking me out again soon.

"Right," said Mum, "if you need to call me you can use Lauren's mobile, it's in the bag on the right. It's four o'clock. I'll meet you at five in the restaurant. Is that all you've got on, just a blazer? Don't you want to borrow a scarf?"

"I'll be fine, thanks, Mrs Stark."

"Bye, then."

Anthony led the chair round the edge of the car park and down a narrow tarmac path that led to the canal.

"There's a cyclist coming towards us and a narrow boat tied up," said Anthony.

I'm not blind. You don't need to commentate on everything. I liked exploring places that I'd never been before. Cyclists tinkled their bells as they approached us. It was magical in the cool evening light with the narrow boats and the sound of the water.

Anthony brought the chair to a halt where the water was gushing over a weir. He sat down on a bench, took one of my sheepskin mittens off and got out the board.

I never knew this was here.

"It's a bit cold," said Anthony, wrapping his blazer around himself. At least his hand felt warm.

Look, a dick.

Anthony looked startled.

"I can't see it."

A duck, lol.

Anthony watched the bird dive underwater.

"That's not a dick, it's a cormorant catching fish."

I watched the sunset reflected in the water which looked like a scene they show with the credits at the start of a film.

"Lauren," his voice sounded squeaky and cold so I knew that what was coming wasn't good, "I don't know how to say this."

He was interrupted by two ladies with Highland terriers which each had tartan coats on.

"Good Afternoon," said the shorter one.

"Afternoon," said Anthony.

By the way, Anthony had put his arm around my neck. A couple of cyclists practically careered into the canal they were so fascinated by the sight of me and Anthony. Conversations stopped and dogs hovered around us looking puzzled.

A younger woman with a black Labrador walked right up to us and spoke directly to me.

"Hello, are you alright?"

"Yeah, we're fine thanks," said Anthony.

She got her phone out and lingered around for a while before wandering on. Wherever I went I seemed to attract attention. Anthony withdrew his hand.

"I can't do this."

Do what?

"I can't be your boyfriend."

Don't you like me?

"It's not that, you're hot, you know that. You're like a beautiful girl who's been picked up in a storm and dropped into a chair."

What are you talking about?

"I can't do it because of the way people look at me when we're together."

Silly boy, he was imagining what people were thinking.

Stop that man.

A jogger in shorts was running in slow motion along the towpath. It would do him good to have a rest.

"Lauren, I can't."

Ask him what he thinks about us.

"I did FC," he said Anthony. The man came right up to us without looking where he was going at all then he carried on past. "I drew some pictures of you, that's all. It's not a big romance."

His teeth were chattering; his breath made a fog in front of his face. Another man was walking towards us in a T shirt and knee length shorts, carrying a sports bag. He was built like a gladiator, swinging his hips because his thigh muscles were so well developed.

Stop this one then.

"No."

You have to.

I screamed. The man put his bag down. His biceps were huge.

"What's the matter? Is he upsetting you?" he said in a deep gritty voice.

Yes.

"Lauren, there's no need to make a scene."

My boyfriend doesn't fancy me.

"What's she saying?" said the man. "What's going on?"

"Nothing."

"Look," said the man, "I haven't got the time." He raised his fist and held it at the level of Anthony's chin. "She looks gorgeous. You take care of her, okay?"

"I do, I do," he said.

"Well it doesn't sound like it. You hear what I say?"

"Yes, I hear it."

The man pointed his finger, picked up his bag and walked on.

See.

"You don't worry about things like I do. It's a different world."

True, I worry about more important things that you have no idea about. Anthony was shivering now.

"Shall we go in now?"

P-

"What are you trying to say?"

Pinch me. Am I dreaming?

Sometimes I had to make up sentences on the spot. Anthony hit the P so I had to think of something. It was quiet between the dog walkers but Anthony had missed his chance. His ignorance and shyness had irritated me.

Let's go inside.

He stood up, switched on my chair and guided me back along the towpath and up the slope to the supermarket and all he said was:

"My toes are freezing."

A gust of hot air met us as we entered the building. Anthony steered my chair into the canteen place.

"Can I borrow some money?"

It's not expensive.

Anthony took my purse and mobile out of my bag.

"Is that you?" he said, looking at the wallpaper on my mobile, a photo of me sailing in the Solent.

Obviously.

"Wow, I wouldn't have believed it."

He could be very damning at times. I thought about our afternoon while Anthony queued up.

Overall I felt warmer towards him because he'd made an event out of the shopping but hardly a minute passed without him patronising me.

He wanted to hide his feelings away so no one knew he loved me. It didn't seem as if he was ever going to learn how to talk to me.

He came back with a steaming cocoa and a thick slice of chocolate cake.

"Ah, that's nice," he said. "Three best inventions: chocolate, heating and supermarkets."

The cake vanished quickly and Anthony swallowed the cocoa in huge gulps. A lady in a white uniform with a hairnet appeared.

"Are you alright, love?" she said, looking at me.

"Yeah, she's fine," said Anthony.

She smiled at me.

"Aw," she said, "is she your sister?"

"No," said Anthony. He didn't say: 'she's my girlfriend,' of course. I don't suppose he'd ever say that to anyone.

The lady picked up his empty plate and went away.

"I suppose you get people checking up on you all the time," said Anthony and turned to look at me. "Ah, you're too hot."

You're so selfish. If you'd looked up in the last ten minutes you'd have noticed that I was melting away. Anthony took off my scarf and loosened the buttons of my winter coat. I could breathe again.

"You've been sweating. Sorry, Lauren."

I liked it when he apologised.

Still, no points for observation or looking at the person you're talking to, Anthony. He finished his drink and picked up the board again.

Thanks.

"You're very polite, aren't you?"

Much too polite, I thought.

Sometimes.

"Did you want some cake?"

There was none left. It had looked nice.

No. I'd cough it all over you.

"I don't mind. You've got to eat."

Aw.

You'll have to do better than that.

"This term's going by really quickly. It's scary."

Mum locked the shopping trolley up and sat down opposite me.

"Did you enjoy that, Lauren?"

*It was ****ing freezing.*

"Oh that's Lauren talking alright," said Mum. "I'm going to get one of those cafetieres and a nice cake."

"I'll catch the bus now," said Anthony.

———

"If you wait a bit we could give you a lift."

"No, it's okay, thanks," said Anthony.

Wait.

I wanted to invite him back to my house so we could talk for longer but he'd dropped my hand and put the board away.

"I must go," he said, "bye, Lauren."

No kiss. Is there any point in loving someone if they don't love you back?

Chapter 13

"Today we're doing a scene from A Midsummer Night's Dream," said Mr Preston.

My hopes rose: a play in room 10D, an orderly peaceful place and a double period of my favourite subject: English. Outside, the friendly blackbirds were collecting twigs to make nests. Inside, the tables had been moved to one side and the space in the centre had become a theatre in the round surrounded by a circle of chairs with a gap for me.

"It's just a short scene," said Mr Preston, "Lauren, you can be Titania."

I felt I'd arrived because he'd chosen me to take one of the parts. Silly, I was like a child in a Christmas play. Mr Preston chose Anthony as Puck and Dan as Bottom.

"Emily?" he said.

"Yes," she said slowly as if she wasn't that keen.

"Would you be Peter Quince, the carpenter? He's the author and director as well as one of the actors."

Mr Preston chose the rest of the cast. It would be strange to see Emily playing an extrovert.

"We start on page fourteen, Act Three. You've got five minutes to read up to 'Enter Peaseblossom,'" said Mr Preston.

Becky whispered the lines to me while everyone else read through in silence.

"Now," said Mr Preston, "Oberon has just squeezed some flower juice over Titania's eyelids:

'What thou seest when thou dost wake,

Do it for thy true-love take.'

We start with Quince, Flute and Snout on stage. Ready?"

They'd just started the play when Anthony danced on behind Emily. The role of Puck suited him.

He crouched down, holding the book with one hand and darted about in the spaces between the actors pretending to be invisible. I opened my eyes and thought: 'The potion isn't working; I can see how full of yourself you are, Anthony.'

Dan left the stage and reappeared wearing the only prop, a donkey mask.

"O monstrous! Oh strange! We are haunted," said Emily and the actors ran off.

"I'll follow you. I'll lead you about, around–" Anthony said to Dan as Bottom.

I tried to stretch my arms and I actually managed to yawn.

"What angel wakes me from my flowery sleep?" said Becky.

"The finch, the sparrow, and the lark," sang Dan.

"I pray thee, gentle mortal, sing again," said Becky. "Thou art as wise as thou art beautiful."

At the end, Dan went beyond the stage directions, flipped up the mask and kissed my neck. I felt hot all over; it was all so public. The class was in uproar. Mr Preston clapped his hands to restore order.

"Very good, Dan. Back to your seats. Now choose one character and write a page about them, including a quote from the play."

I tapped out on the board and Becky copied my words into my exercise book. She read it back to me and I altered a few words here and there.

As soon as Mr Preston asked:

"Who's ready to read out what they've written?"

I raised my arm.

"Lauren?"

Becky read out my piece:

"I feel sorry for Bottom when Puck gives him an asses' head and all the actors run away. He thinks they're joking so he says: This is knavery of them to make me afeared, but people really do shy away from anyone who stands out because they look different."

"That's very good, Lauren, well constructed and a neat quotation. We haven't got time now, maybe we could go into that more in the tutorial group. Anyone else?"

I felt brushed aside though there were lots of hands in the air.

"Emily," said Mr Preston, which was good because Emily hardly ever spoke in class.

She cleared her throat and sat up straight.

"Tom Snout, the tinker, is shy at the beginning of the play but when Bottom frightens all the actors away, it's Snout who comes back on to speak to Bottom: 'Oh Bottom, thou art changed,' he says."

"That's very perceptive," said Mr Preston, "anything to add?"

"I didn't think I read Quince's words very well." said Emily.

"You're not meant to," said Mr Preston, "Shakespeare's having a joke about an incompetent playwright whose lines don't scan. Okay, finally, Anthony."

"Bottom is a big show-off who wants to play all the parts and although people laugh at him he still gets to kiss Titania, the queen of the fairies in the end. He says: 'to tell the truth, reason and love keep little company together nowadays.' He means that people's choice of partner is illogical."

"Very good," said Mr Preston, "from what I've heard you've all done a good piece of work today."

I saw Dan patting Anthony on the back and whispering in his ear.

My hearing was good but not acute enough to pick up what he said. Dan strode out of the classroom grinning.

Becky stood behind my chair to put the books back into my bag and Anthony sat down in her chair and picked up my hand. It felt natural.

I loved the play, did u?

"Yeah, I didn't like the way Dan took advantage of you though."

That made me rock from side to side in my chair, Anthony was getting jealous.

Don't be silly. It's only acting. How was the animation?

"You remembered. It was fantastic, we made a film. I can show you if you like."

Thanks but I'm not good with flickering screens.

"Don't you watch TV?"

Not much.

Anthony lifted his eyebrows a couple of times as if life without TV was unthinkable.

I'm going to the Rest Home after school.

"Rest Home?" He said, "are you ill?"

Lol, no. The biches.

"The Bitches?"

Probably. The Birches on Willow Lane."

"Ah, the D of E."

Yes. Do you want to come too?

Anthony frowned.

"Probably not," he said, "I don't fancy spending eight weeks meeting up with a bunch of old people. Matt and I are thinking of doing something together."

They're just people like you. Someone's grandparents.

Anthony wasn't very open to the ideas I suggested. He always had to knock them down.

Mum says if you came she'd leave the two of us on our own.

"So you mean I'm a volunteer LSA then?"

Anthony was so touchy. He had no idea what it was like spending so many hours with your mum.

Don't be like that.

"I don't like people organising my life for me."

I thought you – oh, forget it.

"Don't get upset," Anthony had noticed my eyes filling up, "Listen, I'll think about it for next week." Anthony went off in a mood.

I'd been dreaming about Anthony coming. We could have done some real talking together. Okay, so it's a rest home but we'd have time together every week for the rest of the term. Instead of that, Mum would be fussing around me. I want to do things with you, Anthony. I want to find out what you think and whether we can grow together.

Mum parked the van in the driveway of the Birches. The tarmac was covered in tiny yellow birch leaves which made me feel sad for some reason.

Maria, a Polish lady with broken English led us through the hallway with its grandfather clock bolted to the wall and the visitors' book on a table. We went through a doorway labelled 'Residents' lounge' which smelt of pine tree spray.

"This is Lauren and her mother," said Maria to the puzzled faces of the old people sitting around the walls. "She come here for some project."

I don't think they understood much of what she said because of her foreign accent. The old people looked a bit shocked at first but once they realised they could speak to me and I could speak back we got on fine. Dot, whose face looks like crumpled up newspaper, told me about starting out in life as a lace maker. She squinted at me, trying to make out my face. I had a game of chess with Arthur. He didn't keep to the rules but he said he enjoyed the game. He sang 'My Way' when it was time to go. Why weren't you there, Anthony? It would have been painless enough.

One day in April, Becky and I sat outside on the bench having lunch and the subject of the canal came up.

"Anthony took you along the canal?" said Emily, "where?"

By the supermarket.

"I didn't know that."

His hands were freezing.

"Why, where did he put them?" said Jennifer.

I'm not saying.

Jennifer laughed out loud. She didn't pick up my mixed feelings.

Anthony's faults were beginning to jar on me. Every time we met he patronised me. I felt a brooding anger at his closed mind, his sarcastic dismissal of anyone different and the way he was so secretive about his feelings.

Mum had a phone call in the evening when I was still up. She brought the phone upstairs.

"You'd better tell Lauren yourself," she said. She put the phone on speaker. "It's Julian."

"I'm sorry Lauren, I'm resigning as your LSA as of now. I can't do it any more."

You can't.

"I have to, listen, I can't take the pressure. I know I'm dropping you deep into the shit but it's the only thing I can do for my own sanity."

Julian always had been a little off the wall which I liked up to that point.

"Oh no," said Mum, "we've got to advertise, interview, get references, do crime checks. Then there's all the training on top of that."

It felt worse hearing Mum enumerating all the things we'd have to do because I knew there'd be problems at every stage along the way: people would drop out, timetables would clash, we'd be spending and wasting money, all that was going to be happening just when I wanted my life to be as simple as possible.

Around teatime on Friday night my mobile rang. Mum picked it up and put it on speaker.

"Hi, is that Mrs Stark?" It was Anthony's voice. He sounded more squeaky than usual.

"Yes."

"Is Lauren there?"

"Yes, she's listening," said Mum.

Listening? I was quietly imploding. I had a sinking feeling about what Anthony was going to say.

"Hi Lauren. Look, I'm in trouble at school."

Mum rushed out the board for me.

What do you mean?

"Something's happened. There's going to be a meeting on Monday afternoon."

Are you hurt?

"No, I'm fine thanks, Lauren, the school will be getting in touch with you. You'll need to be there as well."

I don't understand.

"I can't explain on the phone. I must go."

The phone went dead. Anthony just blanked me out. I was physically sick and then I cried. Everything had gone wrong.

Moments later Trish phoned from the school asking me not to come in on Monday morning because there was going to be an urgent meeting with Mr Hope from the local authority starting at two o'clock on Monday afternoon.

Mum made me a hot drink and brought me downstairs. I watched the garden from the lounge. While I was sitting there, a small avalanche of soot came down the chimney and the room filled with smoky smells.

I had this idea that the previous owner of the house smoked and I felt him in the room with his pouch of tobacco, lighting up his pipe one more time. Mum checked my email.

"This is very strange," she said. "There's a message from Anthony."

I felt instantly anxious. Mum wheeled me closer to the screen. It was just a typed message.

"Hi Lauren, to view my photos enter your password here."

Anthony had videos of rock bands on his phone. I wondered what pictures he'd be sending round. My email address was at the top of the screen and below it the cursor was flashing in a box labelled 'password'.

Mum started pressing the keys of my password. I screamed. I screamed loud enough to wake the street.

"Stop it," said Mum. A row of dots showed that she hadn't yet pressed 'return'. "What's the matter?"

It's a scam. It's not from Anthony. Someone's trying to break into my account.

"Oh my God, you're right. I heard something about this on the radio. They steal your password and send emails to everyone on your address list."

Mum closed the screen down and switched off the computer.

All Saturday, I played Brahms CDs, talking books, I listened to a radio play, I had a go at writing poetry but nothing changed the grinding slowness of that day. Jennifer called me in the evening.

"Hi, Lauren."

Hi, Jennifer.

"Did the school phone you?"

Yes.

"They've asked me to come too."

Monday seemed a century away.

What's it about?

"I'm not supposed to know but I heard something from Mary."

Mary Munro?

What on earth did all this have to do with her?

"Yes, what I've heard is that it's about Anthony being intimate with you."

She rang off soon after that. I turned this over and over in my mind that night. Who'd seen us and what did they see? There were lots of people walking their dogs who might have seen us at the country park when Ant's hand found its way under my blouse or at the canal but nothing happened there.

On Sunday morning I had a long soak in the bath but it didn't refresh me like it usually did.

Becky dried me and dressed me while Mum went to church. I did some reading and Becky turned the computer on.

"Urgent email," she said, "from Anthony."

Let me see.

"I heard about that horrible virus. This one looks genuine though. Should I open it?"

It was entitled 'Sorry' which made me instantly suspicious. Otherwise it looked exactly like a message from Anthony.

Yes.

'Dear Lauren. Sorry about calling you last night. You'll understand the reason on Monday. Talk soon, x Anthony.'

"What do you think about that?" said Becky.

He'd sent a kiss. It was all too confusing.

Phone Anthony.

"Really? Are you sure?" Becky wanted everything clarifying twice over. It was frustrating.

Definitely.

She picked up my mobile, found Anthony's number and called him up.

"It's Lauren," said Becky.

"Yeah, what?" he sounded bombed out.

Have you been drinking?

"Nah, I just can't sleep. You got my - " his voice trailed off.

Yes. What's going on?

"Nothing, I can't say."

Did you know you've been spreading viruses?

"Yeah, everybody's been phoning up and swearing at me. That's what I thought this was."

Poor Anthony. He wasn't dealing with the crisis very well.

Come round.

"To your house? I can't. I've got to go into town. Anyway, that'd be the worst thing to do."

Don't be silly, come round now. We need to talk.

"You don't understand – "

Anthony, I can cope with the truth whatever it is.

There was a pause while Anthony considered this.

"Alright then."

"It's Oak Grange, Landsley Park Road," said Becky.

"What number is it?"

"It doesn't have a number."

"Okay. I'll come round on my bike. I'll be there in about half an hour."

Normally, looking out at the garden in spring would lift my mood. Not this time. The pink cherry blossom and blackthorn hedge did nothing at all to alter my grim mood.

Evidently something very bad had happened. I waited with mounting tension. I dreaded Anthony telling me our romance was over but it seemed strange given the way he'd apologised and sent a kiss. I couldn't work it out.

"Do you want some lunch?" said Becky.

No thanks.

Mum put my chair right by the window. The intercom buzzed.

"It's me, Anthony."

My heart fluttered like a bird. Becky pressed a button and opened the lower gate. I watched Anthony wheel his bike up the ramp and along the path below me. He leaned his bike against the house and stood in a blizzard of cherry petals that the wind had shaken out of the tree. He looked up and saw me.

I tried to wave; I must have looked like a princess imprisoned in a castle. Anthony wandered into the lower garden and peered into the depths of the pond before making his way up to the front door. The intercom buzzed again and Anthony's voice echoed up from the hallway.

"Hello."

I heard his footsteps on the tiled floor. Becky led him up the stairs to my study where I was sitting in the blue armchair. Anthony threw himself onto the settee and covered his face with his hands.

"Oh my God," he said, "what am I going to do?"

"I think you'll have to explain what's going on, Anthony for the rest of us," said Becky.

Anthony muttered something to himself before lifting his face and opening his eyes.

Did you say 'police'?

"I'm really worried that someone's going to phone the police."

Why? What's happened?

"I'm so desperately sorry," he said.

Tell me.

"Someone saw us by the bike shed," said Anthony.

So what? That was months ago.

"The same person saw us by the canal and decided to complain to the school."

They should be arrested as a peeping Tom.

"No, it's not like that. Apparently it's a parent who's claiming that I was forcing myself on you."

That was serious. My mind raced back to the people we'd seen.

Who was it?

"I don't know. The school phoned up Mum yesterday to say it's a 'serious disciplinary matter'. And now someone's hacked into my email account and sent a piece of malware out to everyone in my address book which has got corrupted so I can't contact anyone."

You think it's all connected?

"Definitely. Someone thinks I was abusing you."

But you weren't. I didn't mind.

"Do you think that's going to persuade the police?"

I didn't know what to say.

"You see? It's impossible." He covered his face again.

"There must be something we can do," said Becky. She ran her hands through her hair. I heard a key in the door and steps on the stairs. A few moments later Mum joined us in my study.

"Has somebody died?" she said. "What's happened you all look dreadful."

"Someone's accusing Anthony of overstepping the mark," said Becky.

"What do you mean?"

"A parent complained about Anthony and Lauren cuddling up by the school entrance," said Becky.

I waited while Mum took this in. She put her bag down and sat down in the chair by the desk.

"Anthony," she said, reaching out for Anthony's hand, "I've watched you and Lauren and I think it's wonderful that you get on so well together. You're only young once. You've done the world of good for Lauren's mood and I'll support you against any accusations that anyone might bring up."

That brought a lump into my throat and a moment later I was crying.

I love you Mum.

"I know, love, even though we don't always get on. I want the best for you."

Anthony swallowed, "Thanks. It's good to hear you say that, Mrs Stark."

"So what happens next?" said Mum

"Did the school got in touch with you?" said Anthony.

"Yes, but they didn't say what it was about," said Mum. "Shall I make some lunch?"

"Yes please," said Anthony.

"I'm going now," said Becky, "I'll see you all tomorrow afternoon then."

Becky gave me a hug then she stood in front of Anthony.

"Come on," she said with her arms outstretched.

He stood up and she hugged him tight. It wasn't just me he'd charmed. Mum saw Becky to the door and came back upstairs.

I'd like to sit outside with Anthony for a bit.

Mum took me down in the lift and set the chair on the decking above the pond. Anthony brought a garden chair across and sat beside me. The solar fountain trickled and splashed nearby. I wished I could reach out to Anthony the way Mum had done.

We'll come through this.

"I'd like to think so," said Anthony. "At the moment I don't think I'll be staying at school."

Don't rush to conclusions.

"I don't like all this," he said waving his arm towards my electric wheelchair and the ramp to the lower garden. His voice was different, more human than usual. I felt close to him even if he was telling me things I didn't want to hear.

What do you mean?

166

"All this equipment, the fact that you need a carer with you all the time. Everywhere we go people look at us. Look at how it was by the canal. And now this."

Do you feel sorry for me?

Anthony looked at me and over at the reeds swaying in the breeze.

"I feel – " he breathed out. "This is going to sound silly. You're like a girl in fairy tale."

Go on.

"Like Sleeping Beauty, but you're in a chair not a bed."

Tragic. I'm never going to wake up.

"Lauren, what do you mean? I can't tell if you're joking,"

I'm serious. You patronise me.

"No I don't – "

What do you think about my tragic but brave life? Ask me a question.

"Okay. Do you miss walking?"

I was pleased he'd asked me this, though it was the question nearly everyone put to me.

I've never walked so no, I don't.

"Don't you get fed up with being stuck in a chair?"

Not speaking frustrates me more. It isolates me. I get angry like everyone else does but I can't express it.

Anthony looked at me with fluid eyes.

"With me?"

Of course. Like when you were rude about the older people at the Birches.

Anthony laughed which I didn't mind. He needed to chill a bit.

"Isn't it silly that we're talking like this because some interfering old biddy has stuck her nose in where it doesn't belong?"

It's not a disaster.

"It feels like it. People are going to hate me because I've wrecked their computers."

Just as well you're not going in tomorrow morning then.

"That's right. But I'm dreading the meeting in the afternoon. What can I say? I put my hand inside your blouse: guilty as charged."

And I wanted you to.

"Lunchtime," said Mum, bringing a tray with a plate of sandwiches and drinks, "there's cheese and tomato or ham."

Anthony looked grim when he left us. I heard his bike jangling and the garden gate squeaked as he let himself out. Mum picked up my hand.

"Lauren, I've seen how ill you were when you had pleurisy."

I know, I could have died.

"I want you take risks. I want you to enjoy the time you have."

So I can have sex?

"I don't know about that but I want you to meet boys and have a normal life for a teenager."

Which was sweet but soon I remembered how anxious Anthony was about the meeting on Monday. I just hoped it would all turn out well.

Chapter 14

Mum and I met Jennifer in the car park by the school.

"There's all kinds of rumours floating around," she said, "that Anthony tried to touch you up and that the police might be involved. Is it true?"

Jennifer paused for a moment to catch her breath.

No.

Jennifer looked at me sternly as if she thought I was being naïve. It was time for the meeting to start. Trish came out and showed us into Mr Trimble's office which had a big wooden desk with a tortoiseshell cat bean bag on it. Maybe he had a soft side after all.

The soundproofing wasn't very good; I could hear Mr Hope's deep voice resonating while he questioned Anthony in the Governors' Room. I ground my teeth together while I was waiting. A huge weight of guilt landed on me because I was the cause of all Anthony's troubles. I'd encouraged him. For once in my life, I didn't want to see him. He must hate me. Mum gripped my hand.

"Don't worry," she said, "it's going to be okay for both of you."

That made me feel a bit better but it didn't last. Moments later I caught a glimpse of Mr and Mrs Roberts escorting Anthony past us. I missed seeing his face but I'm sure he was staring daggers at me. Mr Hope followed them out. He put his hand on my shoulder. I instantly felt patronised.

"It's going to be alright, Lauren," he said. "We just want to hear your side of the story."

Mum nodded. I could feel the tension in her shoulders.

"Come along through," said Mr Hope.

Mum guided my chair through the doorway. Sunlight was beaming in, illuminating specks of dust that were floating in the air above the table.

The room smelt stale and sweaty. All the teachers stared at me with grim faces. I felt like a museum specimen. The tightness in my arms doubled and my fists rose up.

"Hello, Lauren," said Mr Hope, rubbing his chin. "This is just an initial meeting to follow up on a parent's complaint. There's nothing to worry about."

Nothing to worry about? What a laugh; just that the only boy who's dared to speak to me is about to expelled or reported to the police or get put on a register so he could never work. And it's all my fault.

"You've met Lauren's teachers before, haven't you, Mrs Stark; Mr Azim, Mr Preston, Mr Todd and Mr Trimble, the head. Is there anything you want to say before we start, Lauren?"

I thought: why are the teachers all men?

Can you open a window?

"That's a very good idea," he said, "it's got a bit stuffy in here."

Trish opened a window and Mr Trimble stood up and stretched his arms out. Mr Todd and Mr Preston followed suit. Mr Hope stayed sitting and twiddled his pen while he waited for everyone to settle down again.

"Now, Mrs Stark, you may have gathered that an allegation has been made about inappropriate contact between Anthony Roberts and Lauren."

Mum nodded and Mr Hope continued:

"The school's involved because the act is said to have taken place within the school grounds, in fact, in the cycle shed by the front entrance."

He cast an eye round the men seated round the table. Mr Trimble wagged his finger.

"Can I just put a salient question to Mrs Stark?" he said.

Before Mr Hope could respond, the head teacher had taken over.

"Did you manage to find the names of any professional people who can vouch for Lauren's use of FC, Mrs Stark?"

He pronounced the abbreviation in a disbelieving tone which made FC sound like a kind of UFO. Mum was instantly on the defensive.

"Not specifically," she said, "there's Marian Henderson."

"Marian Henderson," Mr Trimble repeated, turning towards Trish, "and her position is?"

" - was. She was the senior speech therapist at the Education Authority."

Mr Trimble paused expectantly.

"She had to resign because – anyway, she advises parents and assists at the university and in Fiveways Special School."

"I see," said Mr Trimble in a questioning tone. "And her job title is?"

"She's not exactly employed at all now; she's gone freelance."

"What about all the consultants who've known Lauren over the years? Surely one of them would be willing to support Lauren's use of the board?"

Mayhem broke loose. Mum stood up and shouted and so did Mr Azim and Mr Preston. Mr Preston's voice came over loudest.

"Clive, this is totally out of order," he spat the words out, "FC is the way Lauren's way of speaking, we all know that – "

"Peter, calm yourself. Mrs Stark, would you please sit down?"

Mum thumped the table and sat down.

"I've done a little research," Mr Trimble said, "and I see that FC is not admitted as evidence in court so we have to bear that in mind. The facilitator has a major effect on what's said, am I right, Mrs Stark?"

Bastard. I was furious. How dare he put me down like that? I hammered out the words on the board.

*How else am I supposed to ****ing make my views known?*

"What did she say?" said Mr Trimble.

"She said: 'How else am I supposed to fucking get my views known?'" said Mum with some relish.

"Please, please," said Mr Trimble, "mind the language."

I thought he was going to say: 'because there are ladies present,' but he didn't. I caught a trace of a smile on Mr Azim's face. Mr Hope made a brave effort to restore dignity to the meeting.

"We need to decide on what action to take and whether we should inform the police later today. So, Lauren, can you tell us whether Anthony has ever touched you intimately?"

Never.

"You're sure?"

Yes.

"Lauren, I'm sorry but I have to be blunt here. The allegation is that Anthony put his hand inside your blouse and had his other hand on the crotch of your trousers and that all the time you were screaming in acute distress."

I could barely contain my anger.

What were these stupid people trying to prove? Of course I was in distress. I'd slid down the chair and the pommel of the wheelchair was cutting into my crotch; it was excruciating.

Anthony has never assaulted me. He was just trying to get me comfortable.

"Did he put his hand inside your blouse?"

He asked me first and I said 'yes'.

There was a shocked silence in the room.

"So he touched you intimately in the bike shed?"

Yes, I didn't mind. He put his hand under my bra strap.

I heard someone gasp.

"He fondled your breasts?"

No, not on my tits, at the back.

"Then what happened?"

His hand was freezing. That made my legs go into spasm. Then I practically slid out of the chair.

"It's often some time after the event," said Mr Trimble, "that the victim realises that they've been violated."

I screamed. I was trying hard to explain exactly what happened but he wasn't listening. Mum put her arms around me and tried to muffle the sound.

I was vaguely aware of people standing up and someone leaving the room. I kept on screaming until my throat got sore.

Mum recovered the board which had fallen on the floor.

If I was being assaulted I'd scream louder and longer than that.

All the time I was thinking: 'Why can't you all just accept what I've said?'

I stayed in the room while Trish shepherded Jennifer in.

She kept clenching and unclenching her fists.

"Anthony was always very attentive to Lauren when I saw them together," she said.

Emily and Mary got dragged in and said much the same thing. They'd seen Anthony and me together and I always seemed happy and contented when Anthony was beside me. Mr Azim spoke up about how attentive Anthony had been in the get-togethers.

"Time to sum up," said Mr Hope. "From what you've said, Lauren, and from the evidence of your friends and teachers, I can't see any reason to refer this case to the police."

Thank goodness for that. Let's all go home now.

"Mr Trimble, what's your proposal for dealing with this?"

"We are charged with a duty of care towards vulnerable young people – "

I stopped listening while Mr Trimble rambled on like a vicar about the school's policies and procedures. He got to the point in the end.

"Lauren, your school friends have shown commendable loyalty towards Anthony and all of them testify that your affection is mutual. However, Anthony has contravened the school policy on kissing and cuddling within the school grounds. I propose that we deliver a stern warning to Anthony and that you and Anthony must avoid any contact with each other within the school grounds. What you do beyond the school gate is up to you two but we must maintain the standards and reputation of the school."

It was like a police state.

But Anthony's the only person who does FC with me.

"Until the end of this term," said Mr Trimble, "an adult must be present if Anthony wants to assist you to speak, Lauren."

I wasn't happy about that. The whole point of Anthony doing FC was that an adult didn't need to be there; this was ridiculous.

"And I propose that we should reassure Mrs Munro that there are no grounds for proceeding further – "

So it was Mary's mother who was persecuting us. Clearly her ideas were a million miles from Mum's.

" – we will remind all students at Assembly of the school's policy on kissing and cuddling within one mile of school premises."

How farcical.

"What was that, Lauren?"

I'm glad the committee came to the right conclusion.

Everyone breathed a sigh of relief and I just wished I could have seen Anthony and held him close because he'd suffered a lot on my account.

Over the next few days Anthony avoided me like the plague. He stopped coming to the get-togethers which I thought was excessive, after all Mr Azim was a responsible adult. I guessed that Anthony had decided that our friendship was over and he wanted nothing more to do with me.

Mum took me to the Birches because Julian wasn't about any more.

"I'll do it for now," she said, obviously seeing it as another chore.

I was happily chatting to Dot when who should come through the doorway but Anthony Roberts? I couldn't have been more surprised.

"Anthony," said Mum and she hugged him, "what a surprise."

"Yeah, well, I thought I'd try it out," said Anthony.

"It's good to see you and I hope that meeting didn't upset you too much."

Poor Anthony. He was lost for words.

"Come and sit down," said Mum.

She passed the letter board to Anthony.

"Listen, I don't mind you two being together so if you're happy, Anthony – "

"Yeah, fine, Mrs Stark."

"Then I'll nip out for a bit. I'll be back at five."

Moments later the van was skidding out of the car park in a cloud of blue smoke. Anthony looked around the walls and screwed up his face. He swore at the Duke of Edinburgh under his breath. He took off his fleece top and hung it over the back of my chair.

I love you.

"What's that? Shall I say that out loud?"

Yes.

"You said: 'I love you,'" said Anthony. A sea of faces turned to me.

"You've met Lauren," Anthony said to the lady beside me.

"Lauren?" said the lady. "I knew a Lauren Butterfield."

"No, Lauren Stark."

"Cushie Butterfield?" said the man in the next chair, but he pronounced the name in an outlandish way: 'Boot'a feel'. He launched into a noisy rendering of a song, ending with the chorus which a few people joined in on: 'an' I wish she wor' here.'

"Well done, Arthur," said a man who'd just woken up.

176

He clapped so slowly that he might have been being sarcastic. A couple of women joined in.

"Are you gonna dance for us, sonny?" Arthur called across to Anthony.

He coloured a deep shade of red. "No, I don't dance. Ever."

"Pity."

This is Dot Wood.

"Hello Dot," he said.

"Oh, you know my name, then?"

"Lauren told me."

"Oh, I must be going deaf. And who are you?"

"I'm Anthony."

Dot was a lace maker. She started when she was eight.

"You made lace."

"I did," said Dot. She frowned and looked at her hands. "Worked my fingers to the bone, I did."

"You started when you were young."

"Eight," said Dot, "Lordy me, you've got the gift. Second sight."

"No – " said Anthony, but Dot warmed to the idea.

"Will I meet a tall handsome stranger?"

Hands off. He's mine.

"You'll live to be a hundred," said Anthony and smiled. He was really getting into the spirit of things.

"That's not saying very much," said Dot, "that's only next June. And how old are you?"

"Fifteen," said Anthony.

"Good Lord. And Lauren?"

15 going on 20.

"I thought you were younger," said Dot. "And Lauren said that?"

"She's very clever."

Fuck off.

I hate people saying that about me. Talk to me, Anthony, I'm not 'she'.

"What did she say?" said Dot.

"Shall I tell Dot what you said, Lauren?"

Yes.

"She's a bit shy, she says no," said Anthony.

Bastard.

You are a liar, Anthony. I hate you.

"You young lovers cheer me up," said Dot.

"It's not like that," said Anthony.

F***ing right.

"Oh, yes it is," said Dot. "Trust me, I've been there. That was a long time ago."

"Anthony, would you pass my frame over?" said Dot.

Anthony stretched, picked up the metal walking frame and planted in front of Dot. He can be really thoughtful.

"Thank you," she said. "I've got to make a visit." She stood up and shuffled across the room towards the door.

Anthony made a u-turn with my chair so I was facing Arthur and he sat down beside me.

"Canny chair you've got there," said Arthur.

"It's easy," said Anthony, "you just pull the joystick like this."

He jerked the chair backwards and forwards which made me feel like a tailor's dummy. I frowned and it took a while for Anthony to notice. I didn't like being jiggled about.

"I could do with one of them," said Arthur. "I can't hardly walk and you know why?"

Anthony set up the board.

Coal mining accident.

"Were you down a coal mine?"

"'Ow did you work that out?" said Arthur.

Blue tattoo, my grandpa had one.

"The scar," he pointed to a blue scar on Arthur's temple.

"Aye, that was in sixty five, Camelton," he said. "Terrible, it was, the wall collapsed, five died. I was last out. Everyone hated me and you know why?"

Foreman.

"Because you were a foreman?" said Anthony.

"It's weird," said Arthur. "How could you possibly know that?"

Grandpa hated the foreman.

"It's my friend, Lauren," said Anthony, "Sherlock Holmes."

I'm not yr friend.

"Close the coalhouse door, hinny," sang Arthur. "There's blood inside, there's - "

"Oh, Arthur," said Dot, who'd stepped back into the lounge. "Why don't you cheer us up with one of your happy songs?"

Maria wheeled a trolley into the middle of the room. "You like white tea," and she passed a cup and saucer over to Anthony.

"Yes, that's fine, thank you," he said. "It's a bit strong."

"Strong tea, strong man," said Maria, cryptically, "and for Lauren?"

"No, I don't think she wants any," he said without asking me.

Maria handed out the tea to the residents and the room went quiet with the clink of cups and slurping sounds from beakers. Time for a heart to heart.

How are you feeling?

"Great," said Anthony, "I'd forgotten how much fun the FC is."

He was all smiles, as if that meeting had never happened. I wanted to tell him how patronising he'd been to me.

"Listen, Lauren," said Anthony, "would you like to go out with me?"

Oh my God, a date with Anthony.

Yes, definitely.

"Matt and Emily are going to the see a film on Saturday and I wondered about you and me coming to. It's the new Bond movie."

I was amazed because Anthony had been so distant at school though I suppose that's how he'd had to be.

I'd love to.

"We're meeting up at the cinema," said Anthony.

I was glad Emily would be there too; I wouldn't feel so self-conscious. Mum came in. Strange, I never heard the doorbell ring. Anthony put the board down and stood up.

"Thank you for being with Lauren, Anthony," she said.

He shrugged his shoulders. "It was a laugh, I just had a cup of tea, that's all. I've invited Lauren to come to the cinema with me."

"Oh that's lovely, Anthony." Mum sat down and held my hand over the board. "Would you like to go, Lauren?"

I hate James Bond.

"So do I," said Mum, "but I think you're saying yes."

If it's with Anthony, yes, I'll come.

"It's decided then," said Mum.

"You mean you'll leave Lauren with me?" said Anthony.

"Yes."

"For the whole afternoon?"

Anthony, I love your smile; I wish you'd look at me.

"That's right, you're fifteen after all. What time is the film?"

"I'm not sure, I'll find out."

So it was all fixed up; Anthony would meet us at the tram stop at one thirty.

"You can send me a text when you're on your way back," said Mum, "I'll be at the park and ride."

I didn't mind Emily and Matt being there. It would be heaven: a whole afternoon with Anthony and no adults around.

Chapter 15

I'd spent all morning getting ready. Sylvia washed and blow dried my hair. I chose to wear a pink hairband and a chenille jersey and slacks and the silver Celtic necklace, of course. It rested on my upper chest. The Celtic knot slid from side to side as my head swung about. It reminded me continually of Anthony.

My heart was in my mouth when Mum drove into the tram car park. It was a relief when I saw Anthony and his Mum standing on the windswept platform.

"Hi Lauren," said Mrs Roberts when we got there, "You look well wrapped up."

Anthony put his hand on my shoulder. He's dead shy in front of his Mum.

"It's ages since we had a chance to speak," said Mrs Roberts to Mum.

"I know," said Mum, "I wasn't happy about that meeting with Mr Hope. I'm ever so pleased that Anthony's invited Lauren out."

"Well, it's up to him," said Mr Roberts. "Don't get up to any mischief, Anthony."

"Mu-um."

"I know I should 'just chill'" said Mrs Roberts, "but I can't."

Anthony got the board out.

I wish they'd both shut up.

"Anthony, what did Lauren just say?"

"Nothing," said Anthony, looking up, "the tram's due in one minute."

Mum showed Anthony the shoulder bag with my tram pass, mobile and purse.

He moved my chair along to the disabled sign on the kerb. The tram donged its bell and inched to a halt.

"Bye, Lauren," said Mum, "enjoy yourselves."

Anthony guided my chair through the tram doors and the tram set off. In my daydream he would have sat on the fold down seat and put his arm round me. Instead, he stayed standing up and stared resolutely out of the window.

Maybe this date wasn't going to be as sparkling as I was expecting. I always attract stares from people so it didn't bother me that practically everyone in the tram car eyed me up.

It's only about a hundred yards from the tram stop to the multiplex but Anthony annoyed me by pretending to run into two different ladies weighed down with shopping on the way.

"It's the joystick," he said. "It's got a mind of its own."

Stop fooling around, Anthony. We met Matt in the foyer where Anthony had given me the necklace. My whole map of town had changed since we'd got together. Emily greeted Matt with a kiss. It's easy for her, I can purse my lips but I have to wait for someone to bend down and notice me. Mind you, would anyone want to kiss me when I dribble all the time? Anthony got the board out.

The card's in the right hand bag.

He put his hand in the shoulder bag which hung from the arm of my chair and pulled out the card.

"Happy Birthday, Anthony, love Lauren   xx," he read.

No comment on the kisses I'd asked Becky to add. As he opened the card it played a tune with rising notes.

"What is it?"

Moonlight Sonata.

"Never heard of it."

It's Beethoven.

"We'll get the tickets," said Emily. She and Matt disappeared up the escalator. I called out as Anthony drove my chair between the seats at the sandwich bar. A rough-looking man wearing a baseball cap said: "Oi, watch what you're doin'."

"Sor-ry," said Anthony.

He sat down and stared at the floor as if he was totally embarrassed to be seen with me.

Fat arsehole.

"Don't say that," said Anthony.

I'd expected him to laugh but he didn't. The man looked up and took off his cap. Anthony sat like a statue while the man pointedly brushed past him as he walked out. People came and went.

"FC is magic."

It's not.

Mum tells me I'm facetious. It's just me. Anyway I felt a massive gap was opening up between me and Anthony, which I'd never noticed before. Why was he being so distant with me? I kept telling myself it was only our first date but I could feel him shrinking away from me and I knew there wasn't anything I could do. I wanted to start a conversation but Anthony paid no attention to me at all. Eventually Emily and Matt joined us with the tickets.

"The queue was awful," said Emily. "We've got tickets for twenty past three."

She's become much more smiley since she started going out with Matt. Maybe she's trying too hard to please.

Anthony checked his mobile. "That's in forty minutes," he said. He joined Matt at the counter to choose the fillings for his sub.

"I'm having a breakfast sub," said Emily. "Did you want anything, Lauren?"

No.

Emily had mastered 'yes and no' at the get-togethers. She took off my scarf and put it in my backpack. Why hadn't Anthony done that? For the hundredth time in my life I wished that telepathy was real.

"You're wearing the necklace," she said and picked up the silver knot which caught the light on the edge of my vision.

Anthony was chatting to the girl behind the counter. The tables around us filled up with excited girls talking loudly and joking. It smelt of freshly made bread and barbecue sauce. Matt and Anthony brought back packets of subs with drinks.

"You'll like it, Anthony," said Emily, "they showed a trailer while we were waiting. It looks cool."

Here I was, surrounded by my friends with a film about to start, I should be overjoyed. Anthony sat beside me, unable to take his eyes off my chest. Except to bolt down his sub and top up his drink from the dispenser. Emily picked up the empty cups and papers and threw them in the bin.

"Ready, everyone?" she said.

I felt a bolt of anxiety. Anthony wasn't treating this as a date at all he was just shepherding me about like one of my carers. Matt and Emily went up the escalator while Anthony waited for the lift. Two lifts came and went while Anthony let women with buggies go ahead of us.

Don't make us late. I need people to be assertive with the chair; Anthony was much too apologetic and submissive. When he finally advanced the chair he had great difficulty in manoeuvring it into the lift. He was close to me in the narrow lift but the ride only lasted a couple of seconds and he didn't whisper anything or kiss me. Emily and Matt were waiting for us on the top floor. Anthony and Matt bought popcorn.

We showed our tickets and followed the red LED lights into the auditorium. Emily and Matt went in first and Anthony parked my chair and sat down beside me in the seat at the end of the row. People came in late and blocked our view of the car adverts.

"That's what I'm doing over the weekend," said Anthony.

"What, driving cars?" said Emily.

"No, washing them," he said, "with Jake. Matt and I are saving up for an animation course."

"Sad."

I felt left out. It was too dark for me to speak and Anthony was out of reach.

"It'll be cool, except Dad hasn't decided if he can make up the rest."

The audience was noisy at first but it all went quiet when the opening sequence began.

"I need the loo," said Anthony.

He tripped over my footrests on the way back.

"Are you alright?" said Emily.

"Fine," said Anthony.

"I meant Lauren."

I was fine too.

I think it was an accident but because of the way Anthony caught hold of me by the waist I wasn't sure. When he finished his popcorn he rested his hand on the arm of my chair. I willed my hand to reach across but it hovered like a helicopter in midair and it was ten minutes later when I finally managed to drop it onto Anthony's hand. We held hands during the whole of the bedroom scene. Anthony took his hand away during the speedboat chase before all the fireworks at the end. Anthony stayed sitting to watch all the credits.

"Look," he said, "they played The Moonlight Sonata."

That's right, you do listen sometimes, Anthony. Anthony waited with me on the top floor while people crowded down the escalator and the lift. Soon the bright blue carpet was completely empty of people.

"Look at those lights," said Anthony.

It was dark outside and the building was bathed in blue and green lights that were changing colour continually. It looked magical. Anthony danced about on the carpet.

"I'm going to jump through that window," he said. The film must have gone to his head. He looked both ways.

"I think it's safe," he said, "let's take the lift."

He was a lousy actor. The lift had mirrors on all sides. I smiled at myself. It would have been a perfect opportunity for Anthony to hold the 'close door' button and kiss me but he didn't. He could have prolonged those moments together by riding up and down in the lift but he didn't do that either. In half a second we were back at ground level. Matt and Emily looked up; they were in the middle of hugging and kissing.

Mum could tell I was unhappy when she picked me up.

"What's the matter, Lauren?" she said, "I thought you'd have a wonderful time."

Anthony hardly took any notice of me. It's as if he wished he'd never invited me.

I lay in bed thinking about what had happened. I had such high hopes for the day but it had all been so disappointing. I envied Emily; she and Matt were the shiest people in our class and yet they managed to enjoy themselves. What was the matter? Did Anthony not like the colours I chose to wear? Had he decided that he didn't like me when he got up close?

Chapter 16

After the next get-together, Emily asked to take me round to the nature area.

"Just for a private chat," she'd told Becky.

Sunlight shone through the green silver birch leaves when Emily parked my chair. Irises flowered on the edge of the pond. Emily had changed beyond recognition in the six months I'd known her. She'd found her voice. I'd heard her refusing to go to a film with Matt: "No," she'd said, "it's too crude."

She sat on a log seat beside a red and white painted toadstool. Graffiti covered the marker post, mostly hearts with arrows through them. Emily picked up my hand. A robin sang from somewhere behind me. It was what I had dreamed about before coming to school: talking to my friend with no one else there.

"I watched you and Anthony that first time at the Chinese restaurant," she said. "You've got something special, you two."

Yes.

I wasn't sure if Anthony saw it that way but my hand definitely pointed to the right for yes. I smiled. I was enjoying the sun on my face and the feeling of Emily's warm hand in mine.

"I suppose if you like someone then it's easier to do FC."

Yes.

I laughed. That was true. Anthony would never have finished a sentence of FC if I didn't like him.

"And he took you along the canal."

Yes.

It was beautiful that day, a massive change from my usual boring evenings.

"Do you love him?"

Yes.

I hadn't expected that. My finger pointed without me wanting it to. Anthony made me laugh sometimes but he infuriated me with his ignorance at other times. If he was the only person who took the trouble to learn FC did I have to put up with all the rest: his patronising arrogance, his obsessions and his showing off?

Emily seemed to have picked up my doubts.

"He got you the Celtic necklace," she said.

Yes.

That made me smile. I loved the necklace. But I couldn't forget the fact that Anthony had stood me up. Could he even begin to understand what it was like being me?

"You held hands at the cinema?"

Yes.

Briefly. You don't give up, do you, Emily? My answers were getting repetitive but that's what happens when you're limited to yes and no.

"Did he kiss you?"

No.

"But you did more than hold hands?"

Yes.

We did once and that got Anthony into trouble.

"I'm glad," said Emily, laughing. "Not everyone likes Anthony but I do. A long time ago, it must have been in year six, Anthony stood up for me. The teacher was making fun of the way my head shakes when I concentrate. Anthony stood up and told him: 'She can't help it, it's her eyesight'."

I watched the golden leaves shimmering in the breeze.

"Anthony knocked him off his pedestal. None of the teachers bothered me any more after that. I've never forgotten it. His heart's in the right place. Don't let him slip away, Lauren."

I lay in bed thinking about what Emily had said. Had I been too tough on him, after all I didn't know him that well? Maybe if he got to know me better he'd change. Or was I doing all the work of keeping us going? The Widcombe Rising was in a week's time.

I asked Mum to phone Anthony.

How are you?

"I'm okay," he said, "a bit bored."

Why don't you come to the Widcombe Rising?

"What's that?" I said.

A street party on Sunday next to the canal. They close the road.

"And you want to go?"

With you. You have to dress up as a pirate.

"Yes, are you coming, Anthony?" said Mum.

It's near the supermarket. Mum'll leave us alone. You can keep me safe.

"I think you're quite capable of doing that yourself, Lauren," Mum butted in.

Will you come???

"Yes," he said, "alright then."

At last, Anthony and I can relax at a party.

What's the matter?

I'd picked something up. Anthony sounded uncomfortable.

"I can't say."

Don't worry. It'll be alright.

"I'll bring the van round to your house," said Mum. She wrote down Anthony's address.

I could feel Anthony's anxiety. His angst frightens me because of what happened over Christmas. I thought: 'He's going to vanish at the last moment.'

Who cares what his mum's like? He thinks too much about things that aren't worth worrying about.

I took ages getting ready on the Saturday. I tried out Vicky's nail varnish. She was right; it was perfect for me. I put on the white shirt and the black corset. It was great; it made my cleavage really stand out. Mum tied a black and white polka dot scarf around my head.

We drove into an old council house estate and up a steep crescent, the road that Anthony's house was on. Mum stopped outside and tooted the horn. It was like a child's drawing, exactly as Anthony had said.

"It's gone one o'clock," she said, "he ought to be ready."

Anthony's Mum came down the path and down the steps.

"Anthony'll be along in a minute," she said.

She waved at me through the window of the van and talked to Mum. How insulting, it looked as if she thought I was stupid.

Anthony appeared through the door in a blue and white striped T shirt, jeans and skull-and-crossbones hat.

He fitted a curved rubber sword into his belt. Our two Mums were standing on the pavement.

"Gosh, a pirate," said Mum. "You go in," and she slid open the side door of the van. She carried on talking about budgets and physio and Special Needs.

"Wow, Lauren you look fit," he said. "I'd like to kidnap you for a barrel of pieces-of-eight."

Behind him his mum was saying: "I'm sorry you can't come inside, only we've got steps everywhere."

Anthony banged his nose when I turned my head suddenly. He picked up my hand and the board and waited for me to signal that I was ready.

"I want to squeeze your slim waist," he said.

The keys are in the car.

"Right," he said, "where shall we go?"

To the sea.

I could tell he liked my pirate girl outfit. It's as if the dream he painted had come true. Poor Anthony.

I called out "Oop," which was a happy sound that not everyone recognised. I was drooling down my chin. Anthony stood up to adjust his jeans and sat down beside me, facing forwards as if we were going on a bus journey. My hand hovered in the air, dangerously close to his crotch.

Anthony watched my hand closely. He must have wondered how much voluntary control I had over my movements.

"Well, I suppose we should be getting on our way," said Mum at last.

Anthony's Mum had to poke her nose into the van. "You look so cosy in there. Here's three pounds, Anthony. Maybe you can treat Lauren to a ride."

"Thanks, Mum." He turned to me. "Are you sure this is going to be fun?"

Yes.

"Bye then, enjoy yourselves."

What's the matter with you? Fucking kiss me. I told you before. Weren't you listening? You're just an immature cabin boy not a full-hearted corsair. No one's watching, just a few passers-by and your Mum. My mum would think it's hilarious but you're all stuck up.

Oh My God, Anthony, I'm drooling all over you and I'm longing for your lips to meet mine. I'll pretend I didn't notice.

"Is it far?" said Anthony.

Why does a girl have to make all the running nowadays? If only Anthony would come a bit closer I'd be able show him what I want him to do. Typically, he makes polite conversation. I blame Anthony's po-faced friend, Matt. I can see he's not going to get into the spirit of the Widcombe Rising.

Treat me to the ride of my life, Anthony. I'd like that. Don't go all schoolboyish. And I'm not just going to fall over because you choose to honour me with your presence.

Mum parked up at the supermarket, typed in Anthony's mobile number and tried it out. Anthony's phone played the William Tell Overture.

"Have fun," she said, "I'll call you at four o'clock."

We crossed the footbridge with a band of young people dressed in three-pointed hats and navy uniforms with gold stripes. The blue sky reminded me of when I was seven years old. Barbecue smoke blew across from the beer garden and a band was laying down bad but live rock music.

"Two pounds suggested donation," said the sign at the entrance. When we reached the front of the queue, the security man said: "Carers are free."

"That's cool."

There were balloons and flags everywhere. The shops all had tables outside.

Anthony ran over two peoples' toes with the wheels of the chair trying to get through the narrow gap between the shops and the stage.

A choir of women were singing and swishing pink boas about.

He turned my chair round so I could see the singers and put his jacket on a chair beside me. Then he stood up in front of the chair and looked at me.

"You look – gorgeous," I said.

I leaned forward so he could see my cleavage properly.

"Oh God," he said. "Can I take a picture?"

Let's have a look around.

"Okay."

Why is Anthony staring at me as if I'm a cup cake? *Let's find somewhere quiet so you can hold me.* Anthony led me through the crowd which parted to allow us into a circle around a piano and a man in a peaked naval cap.

"Alright, alright," said the man, "Let's have a volunteer."

No one moved. The pianist with long grey hair played Cuban jazz, switching keys and pace with an elaborate syncopated chorus. Anthony tapped his toe. *Show some balls. Dance.*

Since doing Eurhythmy classes I could feel the power of the music to move my body the way it wanted to go. Anthony acted all nervous, tapping his toes and hopping from one foot to another. *Chill out, it's just a street party.*

"Come on now," said the Captain. "The music needs to take off."

The pianist launched into another stream of notes. The music flowed in circles and someone was blowing bubbles across the clear blue sky.

"Just a sec," said Anthony.

He let go of my hand, stepped into the ring and threw his pirate hat into the crowd.

"Excellent," said the Captain and took his hand. A boy who looked about seven came forward too. "And your names are?"

"Anthony and Seb," announced the Captain.

He led the boys into a kind of barn dance through an arch made of arms. Anthony followed the Captain's moves but added an extra loop. He smiled with his eyes wide. Anthony and Seb looked almost the same age.

The pianist built up the tension and finished with a flourish. Someone threw Anthony's pirate hat back in and he caught it.

"Ladies and Gentleman," said the Captain, "Anthony and Seb."

Everyone clapped. Anthony returned to my chair.

You look great.

"Thanks," said Anthony.

We moved on to a stage where a party of girls were singing.

"This choir," said a man with a flat cap next to Anthony, "come from Chester. Just listen," and he leaned over with his hand by his ear.

Stop letching at me. Hold me.

Why-y do birds sing? sang the choir.

"Oh no, I know what's coming," said Anthony.

Why-y do fools – fall in love?

"I don't know," he said.

I started to cry.

"What's the matter? Did I do something wrong?"

No. I'm human.

He picked up my hand and typed out:

I love you.

Say it.

"I love you."

Tell me something I don't know.

Anthony looked around with a frown.

Anything.

He spelt out the letters with my finger.

"I worry that I'll never grow up."

I laughed and Anthony looked surprised at first, then he laughed too.

"What's funny?"

My finger moved upwards and round until it was pointing at him.

"Me? What's funny about me?"

You think too much. Feel.

My arms pulled him over the arm of the chair. Our lips came close but he pulled myself free.

"I need a drink," he said and he went inside the café and bought some elderflower cordial and rejoined me in the sun. He swallowed a couple of mouthfuls.

"Mm, that's good."

Let me taste it.

"I haven't got a straw," I said.

Let me lick your tongue.

"Lauren, there might be people I know here. I saw Dan."

No one cares.

"I do."

C'mere.

A kind of wrestling match followed and my strong arms pulled him towards me. He let me pull his face closer and closer to mine.

The music, the place, the mood had all got to me and my body moved in the only way it could. I turned my head towards Anthony but accidentally presented my neck. We were dancing in the air and Anthony was coming nearer. Anthony kissed the smooth skin on the side of my neck.

"Uh," I let out an involuntary groan and corrected the position of my head so my lips faced Anthony's and I pouted.

Anthony waited and waited until I guided his head closer still. I reached forward out of the seat so that our lips touched while I was making a raspberry sound. I slobbered over Anthony's face.

He pulled himself free.

"Ow, you bit me," then he noticed my neck, "and I've bitten you."

The End

Things to do after reading Speak to Me.

It's hard to 'act natural' if someone your age is in a wheelchair. Try things: say hello, bring over a chair and sit near them, notice whether they can reach food or a drink, ask before you do anything for them. Talk quietly and assume they understand even if they can't speak. Don't worry if they'd rather be left alone. Volunteer to help people who need someone to read to them or who need help to communicate.

More books to read:
Grace Williams says it loud by Emma Henderson
The Night Sky inside my Head by Sarah Hammond
The Reason I Jump by Naoki Higashida.

Q+A with the author.

When you were Lauren's age, what books did you read?
Fantasy and science fiction, mainly: JRR Tolkein's *The Hobbit*, Fred Hoyle's *The Black Cloud*, John Wyndham's *The Chrysalids*. I read poetry: Gerard Manley Hopkins, Robert Louis Stevenson, and Roger McGough.

What made you write this book?
I went to a birthday party with my friend who's in a wheelchair and one of her school friends said: "I always wished I'd learnt to use the board when you were at school but I never did," that got my novelist brain ticking over thinking about what might have happened. I went shopping with my friend and I felt angry about people's pitying and patronising comments. I wanted to do something about it. I visited a boy of Lauren's age every week for a year to hear about what was happening in his life. The research was great fun and I'm hugely indebted to my helpers.

What's the best advice you've had as a writer?
Read lots: poetry, novels, non-fiction. Write lots: poetry, a journal, short stories, start a novel. Visit book festivals, poetry slams, book launches, meet your favourite writers. Find people to critique your work whose judgement you trust.

Do you have a new book coming out soon?
My next novel is set in the Neolithic Period: *The Way You Move* features Sula, born as a girl, who asks to be initiated as a man.

Acknowledgements
My special thanks go to MM and CM, who started all of this and to MB and SP for being so welcoming. Thank you to Julia Green, Steve Voake and Jonathan Neale, my tutors at Bath Spa University, also to Niki Valentine at University of Nottingham. Thank you, Megan Taylor and all the members of the Fiction Workshop at Nottingham Writers' Studio.